MW00856472

"An artfully constructed,
ing book. A thrilling debut."

—**JAMI ATTENBERG**,
author of *A Reason to See You Again*

"*The Edge of Water* is a beautifully realized epic tale following the lives of three generations of women across two continents. Bankole expertly explores tenderness and heartache without sentimentality. This is a stunning addition to the canon of diasporic tales."

—**MAURICE CARLOS RUFFIN**,
author of *The American Daughters*

"In exploring what happens when we reject our given paths, *The Edge of Water* asks the deepest questions of us.

Olufunke Grace Bankole's marginalized characters navigate heartbreak and hardship within communities that dehumanize them, but Bankole restores their humanity on the page in ways that reshaped me. Despite seeming trapped by adversity, they refuse to passively accept their fates; in this story, survival is not merely a physical question but also a spiritual one. I was gripped by this brilliant and fascinating take on Greek tragedy, employing Yoruba mythology, finding it both humbling and extraordinary, elegiac and inspiriting. Bankole moves from truth to shattering truth giving her characters the empathy and attention we all deserve. I savored every line of the arresting prose and ended this book yearning for more from this incredibly talented writer."

—**VANESSA WALTERS**,
author of *The Lagos Wife*

the

Edge

of

Water

the
Edge
of
Water

A NOVEL

Olufunke Grace Bankole

TIN HOUSE / PORTLAND, OREGON

This is a work of fiction. All of the characters, organizations, and events portrayed in this novel are either products of the author's imagination or are used fictitiously.

Copyright © 2025 by Olufunke Grace Bankole

First US Edition 2025
Printed in the United States of America

All rights reserved. No part of this book may be used or reproduced in any manner whatsoever without written permission from the publisher except in the case of brief quotations embodied in critical articles or reviews. For information, contact Tin House, 2617 NW Thurman Street, Portland, OR 97210.

Manufacturing by Kingery Printing Company
Interior design by Beth Steidle

Library of Congress Cataloging-in-Publication Data is available.

Tin House
2617 NW Thurman Street, Portland, OR 97210
www.tinhouse.com

DISTRIBUTED BY W. W. NORTON & COMPANY

1 2 3 4 5 6 7 8 9 0

For Jonah.

And for the years and faith that led me here.

And imole?
Also the Yoruba word for light.

IYANIFA: IMOLE

THE SHELLS TELL ME SO.
There they are, the five, hands holding like twine. The sixth one lags behind them, his leg dragging as it has every lifetime since the first.

At Imole, the brilliant edge, the souls dwell. Or they pass through, where being is a rest from the life before or the one to come. Olodu—their maker—is in the air all around, splendid like sun through the wings of a dragonfly. Ever on the cusp, the souls come and go, meeting again or saying goodbye. Their bodies are dots of light, draped loosely in cloth—each woven strand a marker of where they have been. *Kindred*, they will call one another, soon or later.

On earth they can be years apart, as daughter born to mother; but at the brilliant edge, the souls are ageless and made the same, as each awaits their turn to descend. Through rounds of life and death, they wait for one another to return to where everything begins again and again.

I am the one who tells you of this.

I am Iyanifa, the conduit of the Oracle of Knowledge, Orunmila. Through him, I see it all in every world—this one below, where I reside, and that one above, where Olodu rules. The six have come with their questions. In turn, I have asked Orunmila to show me their lifetimes. I have tossed the owo eyo in the sweat of my palms, praising the endurance of the ancestors in my breath; in the shape of the shells' landing, answers are divined.

And that is why I can tell you: this time, the order of things will be shaken. The souls will choose their own way, despite what the Oracle has said. Waters will devastate the city of green, purple, and gold. A terrible sadness will drain into the yet unborn. The shells tell me so.

A storm is coming.

Part I

A Line of
Dreaming Women

ESTHER

Shells in the shape of a looking glass

AMINA.

We agreed to write letters, so I started one as soon as you left for America. Yoruba mothers cannot be the only ones who do this: say to their child what should have been said years before, only when it is near too late. Fifty is the age they say a woman is ready to tell who and where she has been; I am forty-six, so I better begin.

⁓

IT WAS JOSEPH THAT I loved.

Your father was not my first choice. It is difficult to tell this to a daughter, but you will come to understand.

Joseph and the older boys on Oje Street ran errands for the alhaji that lived in the lot next to that abandoned bread factory—do you remember it? The big stucco house with the arched doorways and yellow walls, the work of the Brazilian return-ees who had once been taken as slaves. In the afternoons, after school, my friends and I walked the muddy dirt road home. Back then the streets were not so full. We could take our time idling in our thoughts, wondering to each other about the purpose of the latest construction—something was always being built.

The first time I saw him, Joseph was crammed next to Sani inside the front of a faded pickup with tire and metal scraps hanging off the back bed. Sani, elbow out of the driver's seat window, slowed and honked the horn. Like in the films, Joseph's big, happy teeth came into view. Against the shine of his skin, his smile was the most alluring tease. By some instinct, our backs arched straighter. The girls and I pulled and patted the skirts of our green-and-white uniforms the rest of the way home.

For days after, we each tried to catch Joseph's gaze. Loud and forced laughter; hands tightly at our waist to accentuate newly rounded hips. Fifteen years old, we were learning what the older women already knew: a man reads the body first.

"Who do you think he's looking at?" my friend Temi asked.

"Who knows?" I said.

We agreed—outwardly at least—that Joseph managed to look at all of us without really looking at any one. The harder it was to discern, the more anxious we were to know, especially as the end of the school term drew near. Exams out of the way and on holiday, the one that was chosen would have nothing but time to flash her victory in the other girls' faces.

Then one day, as if to settle the matter, in the longest stretch of a glance, I was sure Joseph was looking at me. The other girls must have seen it too; coldness creeped between us.

"Who do you think he was looking at?" I answered my own question with a shrug, pretending even as the butterflies swam up my throat. My friends' silence confirmed what we already knew.

The following day was the last of the school year. For the first time in weeks, Joseph and Sani did not drive by. Lingering as we did on that dirt road, it was all done. I had won the prize of Joseph's gaze, and there was nothing more than that.

⌒

A YEAR PASSED.

On the day Joseph came to Mummy's restaurant, nothing in the air prepared me for it. I have long believed that life predicts itself: before the best and worst of things, a kind of oracle appears. If there had been such an omen on my path, though, I must have missed it. Neither Joseph nor his friends ever came to the restaurant my mother owned. Most of her customers were the freshly-graduated-from-university young men who worked at the secretariat nearby and, every now and then, those with business in the same building.

When Joseph and Sani came in that day, I was counting a roll of cash, a yellow pencil stuck behind my ear. By the time I looked up, one of Mummy's workers had gotten to them for the takeaway order. I moved slowly, not convinced that one look—a year ago—had been meant for me. But Joseph's eyes, the beginning and end of all things, were already on me. Smiling, I felt the cracking of skin at the corners of my mouth. While Joseph and your father waited for their food, I walked over to offer them water.

I wanted to be close to that aura of feeling, to find out if Joseph felt the same. He did. Do you wonder how I knew? At least once in life—maybe twice, Amina—you will know for sure what a man feels for you. He can tell you about it. You can even analyze it with your friends. But nothing will affirm it more than the certainty that springs from the pit of your own knowing.

"How's the work for alhaji? I hear he's running a junkyard." I couldn't care less about the alhaji's business.

"A junkyard? Yes, yes." Joseph waved those words behind him, as if in a hurry to get to some others. He reached for the pitcher I held, and our fingers touched. But it was Sani I saw— for the first time. He rolled his eyes at the pitcher or our hands,

I wasn't sure. He was no match for Joseph, but Sani, too, was handsome. His shoulders moved with ease that surely belonged to an older man.

"Our food's here." Sani pulled Joseph's elbow toward the door. The waitress handed them their bags, and they were on their way.

I waited for Joseph to look back at me. And he did.

But in the days that followed, more than Joseph's visit, more than the touch of hands, I thought about your father. I was drawn to his confidence and troubled by it also—for reasons I did not yet know.

TWO WEEKS LATER, Sani came back to the restaurant. Alone.

"Sani," he introduced himself.

Sani. What kind of name is that? I wanted to ask. It is Arabic, I would learn later. "Esther," I replied.

He moved in jerkily and stood too close. I tried not to look at his legs. He had the polio limp that so many had back then, before the vaccinations.

"Why don't I ever see you in the more interesting part of town?" he asked. "I mean"—he folded his arms and looked around the restaurant—"you would be around more people your own age." Later in the evening, he said, there was a party in the courtyard of that one music parlor. I knew the one.

I prefer being alone, I thought.

He put his hand on my shoulder and, as if in answer to my reluctance, said, "Joseph will be there too."

That was all he said. I promised to gather up my friends and take the bus to the other side of the city.

"Ah, yes, bring your friends!" Sani's eyes sparked with the light of a man with plans.

THE DANFO WAS LATE as usual, not that this dampened our mood. We arrived just as the crowd was feeling good and loose, beers in hand. We walked through the parking lot, through the dancers' shouts over '60s highlife guitar riffs. Sani waved us over. He wore a tight polyester shirt, unbuttoned too far down. "I think he's trying to seduce you," Temi whispered behind my neck, as she walked away toward the music.

I looked around, hoping to spot Joseph.

Sani checked his watch. He turned to the food stands. "I wasn't born yesterday, Esther. I know it's Joseph you came to see." This was the first time I saw your father smile. "You can come with me to pick him up, if you like."

The way Sani drove made no difference to me. Not at first. But after a little while: "I didn't realize he lived so far out."

"He doesn't. I just need to stop by my place and change my shirt." Sani turned to me and tugged on his collar. "I spilled beer on this one and it smells."

I knew then that wherever we were going had nothing to do with beer on his shirt. I knew it, but couldn't say so. There was nothing I could say that didn't sound like doubt, and I was frightened of my own uncertainty. My belly felt tight, like it hadn't been fed for days.

After one minute more, Sani went off the road. He steered down a rocky path towered by drooping trees. He stopped the car. In the instant I reached for the door handle, he grabbed at my wrist.

"Esther. Where are you going?" he asked so gently.

I hadn't thought that far. I turned to the window.

"There's nothing out there but the dark." He moved in his seat, toward me. "Besides, how will you get home?" The sound of his breath filled the car. I understood what would happen then. I'd heard other girls' stories, and there was always one ending. I reached through Sani's arms and turned the radio full blast. If this was going to happen to me, I didn't want the sounds.

I arrived home that night, after Mummy was asleep. I had gone back to the party with Sani, as if nothing happened. Temi, full of drink, hung on his shoulder as he made his way through the crowd, cheerful as ever. Nothing left to do, I danced. I took a swig of beer for the first time. The bitterness stung my gums.

It began to rain. My eyes brimmed, the rage coming on. I was glad for the water washing down the burning.

AMINA

Shells in the shape of sky

IT IS TRUE THAT IN THE END, WE CANNOT TELL THE mind where to go. The storm gusts into the dome, where I wait, the past riding on its winds. Although it is my mother I have loved most, memory retrieves my father first.

⌒

BEFORE I WAS BORN, my father, Sani, was an executive at a steel company; then he lost his job and became a cloth seller. Of the eighteen people who sold fancy-patterned and skillfully woven cloth at Harvest Market, he was the only man, and this, like the limp in his right leg—the aftermath of a polio infection when he was a boy—embarrassed him. When the market's river began to dry, the scraggly children—the ones with snot-stained shirts, food-driven bellies, and no proper home-rearing to speak of—were the first to disappear. They vanished, much the way a street-corner store is found closed one morning, nailed plywood and blank signs where lights and words used to be. Life in the river city had begun to dim.

After two rainless weeks in the wet season, trips to Harvest Market became a scattered, once-in-a-while sort of thing. Even for those for whom it had been a way of life, imported cloth for naming ceremonies and societal weddings was now a seldom luxury. Sani, in his frustration, went days not speaking to my mother and me. In our passing, he hissed under his breath about this person or that one who'd bought cloth but hadn't paid him on time.

One night, at dinner, my mother pushed her questions to him. "You think you're the first man to sell women's clothes to feed his family, the first man whose business struggled in a drought?" I looked at my father. Did he think this? She looked at him up and down, peeling him with each round. He said nothing.

When Sani kicked my mother, she wobbled like a calf in its first step. A boxer dizzied by an unscripted blow, she grabbed at anything near to steady her body. The metal chair next to the kitchen sink and the cupboard handles became like ropes. And in all of this, even with the sparks flashing about her eyes, she stopped to do the numb-tongue-over-sore-gums "Am I really bleeding?" bit. She licked the tip of her forefinger. The taste of blood, like the shock of a first beating, is distinct this way. I have never forgotten.

⁓

ON THE DAY my mother left my father, there weren't any harsh words between them. Sani relished his breakfast along with Esther's pretending everything was fine. Since the rains had returned, he left for the market as usual. The clang of the gate closing meant his Peugeot 505 was on its way. Esther ran to the bedroom closet for the stack of boxes, already filled with our belongings. Until that moment, I hadn't known this would be the day.

And it was good that Sani was gone. Had he been home, he might have embarrassed Esther into staying. He would have summoned the neighborhood aunties to help him shame her.

They would have obliged, warning Esther against being a terrible mother and the perils of singleness.

One day, we were living as an unhappy family of three. The next, Esther and I were in our new flat on Elekuro Street, beginning again. In the middle of that first night, I went to my mother's bedroom door. At seven years old, I was afraid to sleep alone. I watched her stomach and held my breath—my chest aching then, as hers didn't rise and fall as it should. I ran to her side, sure she'd stopped breathing. "Mummy mi!"

"Ehn, Amina, what is it?" she answered calmly as she woke, as if she'd anticipated this childish ambush.

"I thought you were dead!"

The fear of losing my mother is the shore upon which our bond has ebbed and flowed across the years. In that moment, death might as well have arrived. I walked back into the hallway, through the pitch black, swallowed by the silence of night.

ESTHER

Shells in the shape of a wave

AMINA.

Several days after the party, I walked into Mummy's restaurant, and there she sat with Sani. I had not yet told about the night in the car; the fault would have been laid at my feet.

"Esther, come." Mummy waved me to a table by the windows. A woman and a man with fatly folded arms also sat, waiting. I felt desolate inside my mother's stare; the coldness in my legs was instant. "These are Sani's parents."

"No one wants this to become a scandal," Sani's father said, the hint of threat undisguised.

"You know, a girl like Esther, from a good family, with a promising future—why should she be saddled with the reputation of having slept around before marriage?" his wife added, more bluntly.

Your father sat silent, back upright and hands on the tabletop. I stared my disgust into him, willing it like death. My mother pinched my knee under the table.

"So, Esther"—Mummy released her breath—"what do you want to do?"

The casual impression of choice was a trap—"I won't marry Sani. And I wouldn't call what happened sleeping around"— and I fell in.

She sucked her teeth.

"Ah, I see. So he dragged you out of your house to the party. And then forced you into his car." Sweat beaded at the edges of my mother's headscarf. Her nostrils flexed.

The day after the party, Mummy said, your father had gone to his parents to tell them he'd found the girl he wanted to marry. He felt bound to do right by me, he had said.

Someone at the party had seen me get into his car. "Sani was covered in sweat when they came back," they'd reported. So his parents came to meet with my mother to make things right—to agree together that Sani and I would begin a courtship that would end in marriage, once I graduated secondary school.

I raged for many days after. But in the end, I didn't have an answer greater than the weight of our culture. Because I wasn't supposed to be at the party in the first place, because Sani had been the one to tell the story, because I was a girl, I would have to do whatever my mother said. She had face to save and the perception of my virtue to protect. If word spread, my marital future would be shattered.

It was settled, then. Our families would announce the engagement once I graduated.

Life has never let me forget: it was Joseph I wanted, but it was Sani I got. For better or worse, a woman's mate determines the course of her children's lives. It will be the same for you.

Over the next year, I put away my childhood. I stopped taking the dirt road home and rode the bus instead. I agreed to see Sani on the weekends. Rumors that your father and I would be engaged traveled; school became my only comfort. That academic year, I earned the highest marks in my class.

THE FIRST TIME we were alone again, I confronted Sani about the night in his car. He turned to me s-l-o-w-l-y, in that rage-provoking way that you, too, have come to know. My question—"Why?"—was an annoyance, I suppose. But, perpetually tolerant man that he was, he would answer anyway.

"I didn't take anything away. It was you"—he pressed his finger to my chest— "that wanted to go in my car."

"For Joseph." I couldn't remember what it was I had wanted or hoped to have, even with him.

"Joseph or not, I gave you the choice to leave. You knew my intentions and you stayed." The words flowed through his lips, hollow as the air.

"The truth is you forced yourself on me." My words flittered out, confused, as if they weren't my own.

"The truth?" Sani almost smirked. He eased himself into the chair, his weak leg prostrate on the floor. "The truth is I think you would make a good wife for me. And seeing that we don't have a choice now, can you at least give things a chance?"

It wasn't my dream, but it was what I chose: to give Sani a chance. A man may own the children, but it is the woman who imparts the culture. I hoped to give you, my yet unborn, the life I might have had.

⌒

THREE LONG YEARS after we married, I became pregnant with our first child.

"It will be a boy," the river city iyanifa had said. A boy is the cornerstone, so your father and his family were elated. In celebration, they lit four candles for each of the earth's cardinal directions, sealing the foundation a son would help secure. In carrying that baby, I had given Sani the ultimate offering: my womanhood.

Then, one early morning, sitting in bed, I felt warmth slipping down between my knees. I leapt up, embarrassed I'd wet myself. In that terrible instant, something became wrong. Walking past the floor mirror into the light of day, I saw it: my blood-soaked nightdress, like toilet roll hastily stuffed into a bleeding nose.

I gave birth a few hours later. He was like a doll, tiny and soft. His curled lashes shut away the living world. I wondered of the darkness behind them, maybe coaxing him to stay. He died the next morning.

Iyanifa came at once. We sat at the edge of the bed and she held my hand. "That feeling in you, it is longing. And it will stay until you meet him again. It may be in the next life, or the one after that—Olodu decides. But when it happens, you will sense that you have been together before."

Sani and I retreated, separately, into grief. *Happiness*: the notion of the word meant something different then than it does now. Our lives were bound by spiritual laws, the highest being that we would make the best of the hand destiny had dealt. I took the iyanifa's words to heart. From then on, each morning, just as my feet touched our bedroom floor, I whispered to Olodu to send me a child to soothe this loss.

⌒

TWO YEARS LATER, I was pregnant with you. From the beginning, we felt familiar. It would haunt us through the years, in all the places we lived—when we were together with Sani, our time on Elekuro Street. My soul and yours, Amina, strove to understand the lives to which we had agreed.

My mother feared the worst, and so she met again with the river city iyanifa on my behalf. What she relayed back felt veiled. "Esther, we will do whatever we have to do," Mummy had said. "Whichever entreaties we need to make to Orunmila, we will make them. But this child, too, may not live long." The advent of my motherhood had softened her edges. Despite her warning, I knew you would live.

⌒

THE MORNING I DISCOVERED that Sani had another child, I was five months pregnant. I leaned on my elbow to help me sit up in the bed. The harmattan wind swept through the crack under our bedroom door and chilled the ends of my skin. I dug into the tin in my lap and warmed cocoa butter between my palms. Fingers firm, I worked the oil into my face, up around the eyes, pressing out the swollen lids. "Allaaahu Akbar." The early morning call to prayer flowed over the city through the minaret. "Allaaahu Akbar," the muezzin sang. The light voices of women readying for the day brushed against the air like leaves.

Of all the movements I used to see at dawn, I most missed my own during my pregnancy with you. My belly sat like a melon at the top of my crotch. *When you have your own child, you will remember me.* My mother had said this to me, and I vowed never to say it to you. But the instant a woman discovers she is pregnant, she imagines her child's entire life. Inevitably, she thinks of her own mother. You had not arrived, and I wondered if my mother's love for me matched mine for you. I would never tell her that; I refused to confer the martyrdom she had sought.

That morning of the harmattan, I had been awake long before the Fajr prayer filled the city sky. At the hint of sun, your father brought tea and a slice of Agege bread. I was looked after; for the first time, I felt a kind of love for Sani. Each morning, he would bring the tea and bread, and sit at my side before leaving for the office. Those days, he worked at a steel firm and went in early to sort the day's shipping.

Of course, I could have gotten the breakfast myself. But after the baby died, we agreed that I would rest unless it was crucial to move about. In bed all day, I had begun to feel old—joints cracking in strange places. A friend or two would visit and sit with me as the weeks dragged on.

It was my friend Shola's visit that unsettled everything.

"Nooo, noo, no! Stop right there, my friend." When Shola moved through the stories too quickly, I grabbed her hand and begged for the tidbits. Gossip had anchored our friendship since grade school. Head tossed back, jaws loosened with laughter, she was happy to indulge. We shared a love for the drama in others' lives, careful to never reveal our own.

"Good." I said it easily, when Shola asked how things were with Sani. "Things are good." I nodded along with the words as if *good* had always been the way it was. "I even get tea and bread in bed these days," I added, buttressing my case.

"Has anyone else in our circle come to visit?"

"Not recently," I said. "I suppose they're all busy with their own lives."

"Hmm," was all Shola said. Without another word, she moved on to something else—a driftless point about a friend from secondary school we had not seen in years. Hours after she had left, I thought again about her question and the *hmm* that followed.

Later that night, I had a dream: Sani lay in bed with me. He held out his hands, palms facing up. I went to hold them, and then they weren't hands after all. Try as I did, I couldn't see what they were. I woke up crying.

After the bread and tea, after sitting by my side—the sun rising along with the morning prayer—Sani left for work. I slid off the bed and pushed my plumped feet into rubber slippers. I followed him.

For a time, he went the usual way. Then onto the long stretch of road that led to the pier with the fishing boats. I stopped walking. I waited and then turned. He'd gone down the footpath at the edge of the water. He stepped on the pier and leaned on the railing.

I stood under the awning of an herb shop, near a window. And there she was. Her face was hard to see; the black shawl that draped her head obscured any distinctness I might recognize. But her pregnant belly, I could not miss. Sani moved in and out of the way. She talked with her fingers, much like me. He responded with a gesture, first toward the sky and then behind him. I moved in closer, merging into a stream of people on their way to the markets.

I walked by the railing of the pier, trying again to see the woman's face. Sani held her chin in his palm. It wasn't Shola after all. Temi, my dearest and oldest school friend, rubbed his face back. They embraced, and Sani kissed her.

I felt hot in my ears; my legs ran cool.

Just like that, I kept going. Casually, as if I hadn't just seen my husband kissing my friend. I walked past the boats, the outdoor shops and their wares. I kept on, unsure which way to go. At my mother's restaurant is where I landed.

⁓

"WHATEVER BROUGHT YOU HERE must be worth the effort. Come." Mummy pulled me to a bench. "Sit, my dear. What happened?"

I told her about Shola's visit and the strange *hmm*. And then, the dream. When I reached the part about Sani and Temi, she pushed forward in her seat.

"I don't know what I'm going to do."

"To do?" Mummy gathered up her breath. Yoruba mothers are overzealous this way, hurling headfirst into scandal. "Esther, there is nothing for you to do but go back to your husband. If, as you say, he has not abandoned you, and he is even doting on you in recent days, then this is an indiscretion you will learn to forgive."

"Forgive? Temi is pregnant. How can you jump straight to forgiveness?" The biblically promised long life for honoring one's mother and father was not worth the anguish of my silence.

"Esther, please. Calm yourself." She scanned the room and ducked into a whisper. "Think about your unborn child."

"My unborn child?" My face flushed with sweat. "Her father is a liar and a cheat! I never wanted to marry Sani. You forced me, just like him." Then I did the culturally impermissible. I wagged my finger and poked her chest. "What kind of mother are you? You wouldn't stand up for me even when you knew what he had done." My mother shifted in her seat, folding her wrapper tighter to her waist. "You knew."

Her mouth would've appeared to be mocking, had I not known her face; the upturned lip was denial jostling with fear for dominance.

"Hmph." She nodded and kept nodding.

I leapt up from the bench.

"Will you sit there and pretend you didn't know that man raped me? And still. Still, you negotiated a marriage." I sucked my teeth. "I hope they paid you a dowry worth your daughter's dignity."

And just as I reached the door, I heard it.

"When you have your own child, you will remember me."

Even now, I see my mother on that bench, shaking and small. Nothing she had said was new. Acceptance of infidelity was the cultural way. And what Sani had done might have been wrong, even deceptive, but certainly not *rape*. For years to come, my assertion that my mother had failed to defend me against rape would be what upset her most—not my experience of it.

⁓

SANI CAME HOME, no differently than the days before. Shoes off at the door, workbag on the table. He unbuttoned his sleeves as he walked into the parlor where I sat, waiting.

"How was work?" I was ready for the fight.

"Nothing eventful." He sat next to me and leaned back on the sofa, hands behind his head.

"Nothing?"

"No. Well—" He frowned. "I mean, there was more paperwork than usual. Some new bureaucratic mess, the same as always."

I nodded, withholding any hint of feeling. "Even when you met Temi at the pier?"

He sprang from the sofa and grabbed at his head, almost forgetting himself. And just as swiftly, the panic gave way. "Esther, you know I've always been direct, I never—"

I only wanted the truth.

He wiped his face. *Things*, he called it, had happened a few times.

"When?"

Before we were married. And then again after the miscarriage, he said. "So, what now?"

"I don't know how else to say it, Esther." Temi was also pregnant, as I already knew. Further along than I was, he said, and about a week from birth.

Adultery can be pretended away, but a child?

I threatened to leave. What else could I do? But the thing is, Amina, a threat is only as good as one's willingness to carry it out, should conditions go unmet. I wasn't ready to leave. Not then.

As though we were business associates, your father and I negotiated the terms of our marriage moving forward. At the meeting with our families, we reached an agreement. Sani would make an apology to me and my mother for his indiscretion—a formality meant to restore honor to the aggrieved. And because I had to live with the actuality of his mistress and their child, he was to stop seeing Temi publicly.

⌣

ALL WAS NOT LOST, Amina. Life still yielded sweetness.

One day, after thinking too much about everything, I went into our yard, pulled down my pants, and squatted. I placed Sani's chew stick on the ground between my legs and trickled hours-held urine on it until the dirt steamed. I put it back where he would retrieve it to brush his teeth.

When I became bored with the chew stick, I began mixing urine into his palm wine. One night, he called me into the kitchen to ask where I got the wine.

"The same place I've always bought it." A roadside stand that shipped it in from the village.

It tasted different, Sani said. If he thought I was up to something, he didn't let on. I think he was too arrogant to suspect I could be that cruel; or maybe he was afraid to confirm I was as wicked as his family had said. He sipped from a cup held loosely between his fingers. "It's good."

⌣

TWO MONTHS LATER, you were born. I took well to being a mum, even early on when I feared I might drop you on your head. Mummy came to do the cooking and washing when she managed time away from the restaurant. Your paternal grandmother should have been there too, but given the part she played in my marrying Sani, I didn't want her anywhere near.

Once, when the house girl left our gate open, Sani's mother came through the courtyard and pushed her way into the kitchen. I locked the bedroom door and wouldn't leave. For more than an hour, she sighed and shifted noisily on the sitting room sofa. She finally went home when the house girl said she needed to go to the market. My refusal to welcome Sani's mother sharpened the wedge between me and your father, and between me and my own mother, who said I had disgraced the family with my stubbornness over the past.

Sani was not disappointed that you were a girl. Like all the men I had known, he had praised the virtues of having a son as firstborn. And yet he was happy that you came. And he was happy for your sister, Oyin, too. When you got older, he would drive you and Oyin in his Peugeot, to let the world know he was a father of two. "Children are a man's wealth," he said.

Sani sent money to Temi, though he never mentioned it. But our town was small. The tale-tellers clamored to tell me how it was going with Sani's other family. One said that though Temi was satisfied with her monthly stipend, she was certain that Sani remained with me because I had bewitched him. I wish Temi knew—and I would have been glad to tell her—that your father was hardly worth the effort of my witchery.

⁓

IN THOSE EARLY YEARS, before you formed memory, before the years at Harvest Market, Sani held himself firm and assured. He was the head of operations at Ni-Co Steel Manufacturing.

During the 1970s oil boom, industries that created drilling and production materials exploded. Your father's lucrative job meant we lived the good life. And it showed. In our garishly ornamented house, for one thing: the imitation Corinthian columns that flanked our gates were embarrassingly out of place, as were the appliances from overseas that sat mostly unused. We had the glow of people life treated kindly. Still, I set aside for a stormy day.

On the afternoon Sani was laid off, I came home to him sitting at the dining table, head in hands. Four Guinness bottles—three fully empty—stood in formation, announcing the order in which they'd been drunk.

"Esther?" My name, a burp, and a smile as deep in his jaws as crying: all came out at once. He lunged at the room. "All of it"—he pushed his chin into his chest—"you better enjoy it now. It's all going to hell, everything I worked for, all of it." He scrunched his lips and swatted my purse off the table. "No more designer this and that for you, hehn?"

He tumbled into darkness that shrouded him fully. I didn't worry too much. As long as I had known Sani, he had worked. We had the things we needed: you, me, and everyone he loved. That was his way.

But then longer and longer, he lingered in bed. My coaxing or pushing provoked his rage. By then I'd begun working again at Mummy's restaurant and selling off the nicer pieces of my jewelry.

"I can't take just anything." Friends would mock him, he said. And so he waited. What was he waiting for? "For something proper to open up." He scratched himself through days-worn house clothes. "Something always does."

Of course, nothing materialized. Except—for me—regret: that I had hitched my youth to a man who couldn't give me the love or life I wanted. I would have hated to hear this from my own mother then, but it is true, Amina: every choice you make, even in your girlhood, will have a hand in the woman you become.

~

I BEGAN TO PLAN. I combined years of pocket money with the sum I had saved from working at the restaurant. By the time you turned seven, I decided to rent a two-bedroom flat; one room for me and one for you.

"Think about what this will do to your child," my mother warned, when I told her about the flat. "I agree he shouldn't be beating you. That is not a good thing. But is this the only way to resolve the matter? You need to consider your own part in it."

My mother was unmoved by Sani's years of abuse, which began just days after you were born. A beating here and there, for her generation, was not enough to leave a husband over— especially the father of one's child. With genuine effort, anything could be talked through.

"It's simple," I told her. "If you go against me, you'll never see us again."

"After everything I have done for you, you're talking to me this way?" She slapped her palms together and sucked through the gap in her teeth. "And you are taking Amina away from me."

I closed my eyes and searched the dark for words. "I'm leaving Sani."

On the morning of our move to Elekuro Street, my mother sent a young man, her house girl, and a truck to help haul our boxes away. When we arrived at the new flat, it had been cleaned and furnished with all the necessary things: two sofas and a center table in the sitting room; a mattress and sheets in the bedrooms; plates, cutlery, and pots in the kitchen.

Two days later, Mummy gathered three of her brothers and their wives to meet with Sani's family and negotiate our divorce. He would remain in our old flat in the river city, which was just fifteen kilometers to Elekuro; if he wanted, he could visit with you. And so long as he sent money each month, I agreed, the world would hear nothing of the rest—at least not then.

AMINA

Shells in the shape of god

AFTER MY MOTHER MOVED US TO ELEKURO STREET, A
year went by before I thought again of my father.

She had built for us a world full of just me and her, and
our days in the flat come now like flashes of thunder in warm-
ing skies: Esther sleeping in a room across from one in which
I could never sleep too well. In the night, a stray dog stub-
bornly barking outside my window. Into the mornings, waves
of love songs from Indian films on my mother's telly tingling
my ears—each weeping note swimming through a hallway that
held captive in its cracks the fatty aroma of the spinach and
dried fish stew she had cooked hours before. Once in a while
she sent me, alone, to a corner market for something small, like
oil to fry akara. The flat was shabby next to the one we'd shared
with Sani, but it was ours—together.

All of this notwithstanding, I was sure my father's absence
must've had to do with me.

"In our culture, men own the children," my mother once
said.

"Even the ones they leave behind?" I had asked.

"Yes, even those."

"So where is he then, Daddy?"

The following evening, she took me back to my father's house; he'd finally asked to see me, she said, after many months of absence that hadn't made his heart grow fond.

"Only for a visit, Amina."

But while I sat in their parlor, Sani and his new wife, Lara, brought me foil-wrapped sweets and a large Fanta. So I begged my mother to let me stay. Determined as she was when she left Sani, she believed what the culture said about who children belonged to. Besides, she said, school was out, so I could stay for the next two months.

⌒

I LURKED ABOUT MY old home, dodging the shadows of my stepmother Lara's presence. Even with my eyes on the past, I cannot conjure her face. Being afraid, though, my body recalls; I hold my breath at the memory of it.

"She's an easy girl," my father said to Lara, about me, from outside my bedroom. "You can think of her as your own daughter."

"Whatever you say. I won't care for a scraggly head of hair on a child from another woman's womb." Lara shaved my head into the pit of a tin bowl. She sucked her teeth and spit onto clumps of black, oil-shined hair. By the next morning, yellow-green pus crusted the nape of my scalp, where the rusting blade had scraped mercilessly. After Sani left for work, Lara put bread and a cup of chocolate on the dining table. She locked herself inside their bedroom.

I ate quickly and ran out the door. I unlatched the gate and strolled the dirt path that joined our compound to the thoroughfare. At the sweets and biscuits stand, I stopped to dig in my pocket for change. In the shop next door, a tailor—tape rule around his neck and a teethed pencil in hand—blasted a tiny metal radio that rode into static and out with sound. When the music tuned in: "Baaaby," a man sang. America came to me first through its rhythm and blues. The man's cries, as if telling of now, of the storm, compared his love to a boat drowning. I closed my eyes and saw an America I might someday reach. There was a feeling to it, wide like the morning air.

A FEW WEEKS INTO my stay at my father's, my stepmother decided that Esther had left me there to perform witch-craft. Lara had tried to get pregnant and miscarried each time. To all who listened, she proclaimed me a sorceress in training—my mother's little helper, there to set the curse to leave her barren. And so, on three consecutive Sundays, we attended Confessions Holy Church. Kneeling inside a circle of tongue-speaking women draped in bleach-white gowns, with a child's giddy imagination, I related in detail my and my mother's plot.

Soon after, I was taken about, recounting these schemes that in truth were never hatched. Full-breath sighs, disbelieving headshakes, and O-shaped mouths met us at each home of family and friends—some my mother's, others my father's.

"Now, Amina, repeat to the elders how your mother plans to eat my womb alive," my stepmother demanded. "Tell them how you stare at me as I sleep, summoning your witch-bird totem to come for my unborn child. Tell them!"

Sani's new wife begged the elders to cajole me to release her womb, whatever it took. So began the entreaties to appease the curse through me: a new stringy-haired white baby doll, a slightly used bicycle, and two square bottles of sparkly fin-gernail polish. At home or play, little children understood that newness was near richness. And wealth, if it couldn't be had here, might be possible abroad, I thought. In my father's house,

I was a step closer to the America I'd begun to perceive—a lavish home with overflowing toys and treats in every room. On the telly shows from overseas, this was how American children lived—indulged at every turn.

With the discipline of times-tables recitation and the storytelling gift of a child who had lived before, I turned each adult's suggestions into a layered tale of witchery that had never taken place. The door of the tiny rundown flat I shared with Esther had swung boldly into a universe of barely used toys and pushed me to talk and talk about things I didn't really know. But these claims didn't bring me nearer to Lara's love; she shunned me all the same, locking herself away each morning, as soon as the gate closed behind Sani's Peugeot.

THE DAYS WERE LONG, but the months passed quickly. I waited and nothing came. Then, as when fire is reignited under a near-boiling pot, my feelings began to gurgle. And finally: shame. It crawled from my stomach and choked my chest like the bitter rise of unsettled food. The lies splattered up, soiled everything.

One morning, I woke up restless in my limbs. I washed my face, brushed my bald head, and cleaned my teeth with the antiseptic chew stick. Ogi still warm on the dining table, I went to my stepmother's bedroom to collect my breakfast money. I escaped.

I took the akara money and ran to the only bus station I knew—the one past the burnt grass field, catty-corner to the tailor's shop, next to the abandoned bread factory. Skinny eight-year-old legs, sprinting like a frenzied ant, scraped the shadows of the akara stand and tore in the direction of idling buses. Past neighbors' homes, the fruit-and-plantain woman's stall, and the old albino man who sold sweet colored water in clear plastic bags, I ran. To the jingling of coins in my shorts pocket, I ran still, through cramped back roads, zigzagging the edges of muddy ditches. My throat: a wheezing hose spitting into the humid morning air.

When I arrived at the flat on Elekuro Street, my mother was away at work. She came home to me sitting inside the entranceway, toasted a shade darker by the late afternoon's pigment-pounding rays.

Palms clasped, Esther bent forward and grabbed at her chest. "What in god's name are you doing here, Amina? Why aren't you at your father's?" She held my chin, turned my face to the side. "And what the hell happened to your hair?"

I wanted to lie. But I admitted that it wasn't my shaved head that made me run from Sani's house. After the bumps had peeled, the prickly boyishness of my scalp and the Yoruba face it revealed were quite becoming, I'd decided, and with a shrug, too—as children do to calm the sting of rejection. I'd held a quarter piece of a broken hand mirror to my face, turning back to front. *Fine gal, so fine sha!* Back tightened, shoulders down, I became like the Kenyan girls: the ones in that glossy geography magazine who posed with a too-wide smile, a Fanta in hand, and a collared-shirt, khaki-clad white man. With this new head, I fit right in with the uniformed schoolgirls who walked past my father's gate in the late afternoons. Amid everything— the lies I'd told and the stories that were only half true—my bald head was the firm thing.

"Mummy, they said you're a witch! That is why I ran."

⌒

"HER MOTHER SNATCHED HER shortly after 1:00 PM, while her father was at work," they began to say. The talk of neighborhood gossips reached my mother and me a day after I'd escaped from my father's home. The busybodies, we were told, had trickled into Sani's yard and exchanged sworn—and some even claimed, firsthand—accounts of the abduction:

"Ah ah, if I am lying, may god not let it go well for me!" one shouted in the direction of dubious bystanders. This one snapped her thumb and middle finger up toward her face and down to the back of her neck—a symbol of divine invocation.

"Enh henh. I'm telling you what I saw with my own eyes. She strolled through here with her arrogant self, her chin sitting inside her neck like a roll of coins. Abi she is the first to divorce?"

"That little girl followed so obediently, shuffling behind the witch, clutching the tail of her wrapper. She was crying for her father, you know. The woman has no fear of god, I tell you," a third said.

That my mother had no fear of god—of anyone, it seemed—is the grievance our culture would never forgive.

⌒

WE HAD TO LEAVE Elekuro Street quickly, Esther decided. The tales were already spun, and the elders would believe the lies. "And why not? I am a woman, after all," my mother said. An educated one who thought too much of herself. "Certain things are not so easily resolved. Even with the most earnest denials."

She grabbed our clothes and whatever else could be bagged, and tossed them into plaid canvas totes. Unlike the women in the old neighborhood, the aunties here would not shame Esther. By the time we finished packing, two or three of them stood at our door with plastic containers of food and bottled drinks for the road. We left Elekuro in the middle of the night, in the back seat of a neighbor's car.

ESTHER

Shells in the shape of a wheel

AMINA.

If nothing else good can be said of me, I know how to pick up and go quickly when circumstance demands it. Moments before we left Elekuro Street, while you slept on the parlor sofa, I went into the bathroom and ran the faucet. I sat on the cement floor and wept. I should take you again to your father's and return home to Mummy, I thought. And just as quickly, something reeled me in. Amina, may you never be so worn as to teeter at the edge of hopelessness.

After we left Elekuro, I vowed never to run again—not from Sani, not from the tale-tellers, not even god himself. Although we moved to a street that intersected our old one at its center, There but for the Grace of God Go I Avenue stretched many kilometers from our former neighborhood, towns away from anyone that knew us. This, Amina, I swore, would be our last home.

There but for the grace of god go I is what we say when we are secretly thankful another's lot is more terrible than our own. This street has certainly had its dramas and reasons for caution. But I saw myself here—having everything we needed, finally. Once upon a time, I thought I might have a career in science. I was such a bright girl. Can you imagine, Amina, your mother

34

as an engineer or even a biologist? Where might we be now? There comes a point when one must relinquish the dream for the chance to make the best of reality.

Like all the mothers in my lineage, I have sacrificed myself for the sake of love. After I was accused of witchery, Sani stopped sending your monthly allowance. I, alone, paid for everything. I stayed home from work when you fell ill with malaria. I turned down courtships with influential men—ones who would have funded my way through life—so I could raise you in peace.

Lifetimes have passed since the night of that party. Still, I cannot help thinking I cut short my future by going with your father in his car. Others' betrayal is a part of living, that is true; but it's betrayal of yourself that is the hardest to forgive.

⌒

TWO MONTHS AFTER MOVING to There but for the Grace, I ran out of money and could not afford your school fees. Business had slowed at my mother's restaurant, and there were not enough work hours to go around. I reached out to my old friends—Shola and a few others. It was then I learned a woman must know the sort of friends she has; not every one is for every thing. Some friends, like Shola, are for entertainment and gossip. Others are for giving and receiving advice. Then there are the rare and precious friends who you can run to in times of trouble and be your entire self, unpolished. As it turned out, in my moment of desperation, I did not have any of the latter kind.

I sold my clothes and jewelry as I had done in the past. With that, I managed our groceries and your school fees. Still needing to pay rent, I did what I saw my own mother do when fate dealt her the same: I began catering events and celebrations for money. Within weeks, word spread about the quality of my cooking. It helped my case, too, that my mother's restaurant had always been popular in the area. For years, I worked and saved. And then Mummy retired; she gave me all her equipment, recipes, and information for suppliers. Even with that, it took several years more to buy the space that is now Esther's Palace.

Amina, I have a point in all this: you always have yourself. When help is exhausted and hope is low, you can seek your own heart for what comes next. You might find that everything you need is already with you. However you feel, you are never bereft.

It could be that the residents of There but for the Grace looked to me as an example of what they hoped to dodge. It was no matter; I was satisfied that I was doing my best. On the third anniversary of opening Esther's Palace, I wore my prettiest dress—the purple one with the lace trim—and my highest heels. I took a taxi downtown to a car dealership and asked to look around. Of course I didn't have money for a new car, but I certainly had the mind to dream. I opened the driver's side door of a bright white Volkswagen Beetle and sat inside. I gripped the steering wheel with both hands, leaned into the windshield, and peeped into the future.

AMINA

Shells in the shape of a rock

MY MOTHER'S SCREAM—LOUD, THOUGH NOT UNEXPECTED—
pierced the lull of early morning rains. Rainwater pounded our
flat's corrugated roofing; it would trickle down cracks in walls,
form a puddle on the pavement, and become an eager stream
that led to the main gutter on There but for the Grace of God
Go I Avenue. Whatever else was said about the goings-on on
our new street—that gossip moved faster than the mouths from
which it came; that neighbors smiled in each other's faces but
wished one another ill; that you couldn't trust your man in the
vicinity of Madame Lawal—seven years after we arrived here,
There but for the Grace still had a kind of calm: one that let you
sleep with little concern about what, if anything, was happening
elsewhere.

I realize now that I have not slept as well since. All around
the dome, eyes are watchful. Bodies are alert and ready to
depart, should help come.

That morning, before the scream, I'd been awake an hour,
breathing alternately with the buzzing of my sister's nostrils.
Years after Oyin came to live with us, despite my nightly com-
plaints, her low-pitched snoring continued to hum through
the bedding. I stood up on the mattress, stepped over her bared

breasts, leaned into the wall, and rested my chin on the window ledge. Through a filmy stream of netting, I watched my mother. One hand gathered the bottom edges of her nightgown and tucked them between her thighs; the other massaged her chest and patted it: *one, two, three,* as if relieving some knot there. She pulled at the roots of her hair.

Her voice, whatever she said just then, came through the window as a groan. She dropped the hem of her nightie, slapped both hands on her head, and paced around the car. The once-white Volkswagen Beetle was covered in runny brown lumps.

"They've done it," she said to me as I walked out the back door. I didn't respond. I wasn't expected to.

"They have finally done it, Amina. They want to chase me out, but I won't go." We stood there, in matching nightdresses, facing her new Beetle. Feces slid down from the roof of the car, draping the windows and doors like a shaggy palm tree. "They must have come during the night," she went on. "Only god knows how they got over that fence." Broken pieces of beer-bottle glass were set within the top edges of the concrete wall that enclosed the front and sides of the flat.

"Who knows?" I said. "Maybe they came through the alleyway." My mother looked to the back of the flat, toward the outhouse. "Hmph. Of course." She shook her head. "Where else would they get all of this shit?"

The rain, still steady, hadn't rinsed the Beetle clean. It was just enough to dilute the heap on top of it into a weeping mess. And even through that rain, the sun, already much too hot for that time of morning, had begun to peek through. Everything melted and dripped, and white flakes of the car's paint went along with it. Whatever else was intended, at least this damage had been done.

The inside of the car, too, was full of it. Esther opened the driver's side door, and the stink of weeks—maybe years—old waste pushed up our nostrils. Houseflies swarmed; the high-pitched buzzing tickled behind my ears, my inner thigh. The clouds melted at the sun's urging, and the rains came to a sudden stop. My mother threw her hands into the air, hung them again at the sides of her neck, and twisted from side to side.

In soaked nighties, we walked to the back of the flat and filled plastic buckets with a hose that stretched out from the bathroom window. With back-and-forths of my lanky and her flabby arms, we washed the Beetle down. Undigested pieces of corn, and other things that had been consumed by the defecators, fell to the ground and reluctantly washed into the gutter. A splotchy mix of white, gray, and various in-between shades remained on the car.

⌒

"YOU KNOW, ESTHER IS the first woman in this neighborhood to own a new car." On There but for the Grace, this was immediately said when a stranger discovered the driver of the white Beetle was my mother. "Most of these men don't even own one," they might say. Not Rufus, the electronics repairman who, whenever asked about business, responded too quickly that it was flourishing and things couldn't be better. The better-off-by-association-only residents of the street were also without a new car—like Madame Lawal, the aging coquette, who well into middle age remained the standby of married politicians, rich chiefs, and other important men. Madame Lawal was one of those women whose beauty could be gauged simply by the way other women spoke of her. They would say *She's so damn full of herself* to mean she knew quite well the extent to which her looks carried her through life, and was not sorry for it.

Niyi, though, owned a new car. Niyi, the young-looking-but-undoubtedly-much-older-than-he-let-on neighborhood flirt, the ridiculously handsome man by whom all of us girls—young and old—were tenderly weakened. The mystique, if there was one, might have been his warm laugh and upper-teeth gap, the kind that—it was said by the knowing women—belonged only to men who turned stone into manna in the bedroom.

～

THE MORNING AFTER my fifteenth birthday, Esther sat me at the edge of her bed and kneeled on the carpet.

"Do you know what is meant by *sweet banana*?"

Several years earlier, before I knew much of anything, King Sunny Ade had released "Sweet Banana," to the delight of juju music fans who craved a little sexual banter with their drumbeats and who admired his willingness to satisfy it. His voice—the slipperiness of it, they'd said—was a kind of penetration: it pushed through that missile-shaped throat so effortlessly, one wondered of other marvels the King could deliver.

"No, not me," I said. "I don't know." I'd learned to say no to the things that would have broken my mother's heart had I known the truth of them, which in this case I did. My silence assuaged both our fears.

"Well, the good news is you won't find out anytime soon." She pressed down on my knees as she rose, squeezed them together, shut. "Don't let me catch you near that Niyi or the likes of him. If I as much as smell him near you, nothing good will come of it. Try me."

Esther, like the other women around her, believed she could tell if her daughter had had sex by smelling and then tasting the lining of her panties, or watching the way her hips moved when she walked. "The sex"—she'd said it just like that, as if it existed unto itself—"lingers in the stitching." So, after a day out with friends, my sister, Oyin, only several months older but eternally more mature, would walk straight from the sitting room entrance to the bathroom, slip off her underwear, and hand it to my mother, who stood outside the door.

Oyin's hips soon gave everything away. She had become careless; likely succumbed to the butterflies—that bottomless tightening and loosening of the gut at the remembering of a lover's hands. Late that December, she'd begun to walk with a switch and a widened stance. The night Esther noticed this, Oyin had come home from a date with the boyfriend that should never have been. And she must have forgotten the clean panties she'd hidden inside her purse. I already knew the scent of sex and smelled it on her for the first time just then.

Esther must have also smelled it, but said nothing. If my sister sensed the strangeness of my mother's silence, she didn't show it. We cooked dinner and she moved around the kitchen too freely, carrying on like a drunk in a field of mines. The aftereffect of sweet banana, I supposed. Esther watched, head cocked to one side as if on the one hand awed by the unfolding, and on the other daring my sister to continue the charade.

Even after we cleared the plates and began washing, my mother sat and stared in that same way. Squinty eyed, she followed our fingers, our elbows as they reached over and around her to collect leftovers of rice, fried plantains, and goat meat stew. Then, as if to get up, she palmed the corners of the dining table. But she remained seated, shaking her head. And though she looked nothing like him, it was him just then: Sani in his simmering rage, the first time I saw him beat my mother.

Suddenly, Esther was behind Oyin. She reached around her waist and rinsed her hands in the soap water. Her crotch to my sister's backside was like that invasive swivel of a man's hips to your groin when you'd rather be dancing some feet apart. She wiped the bubbles on the back of Oyin's dress, then rested her hands there. Something began to shake. Oyin's legs or my mother's hands. I couldn't tell which. The glass cup Oyin had been washing over and over and over, while Esther stood behind her, plunged into the sink.

"Meet me in the bathroom," Esther whispered into Oyin's neck. My sister did not scream. What came out was more like a gasp—the kind that follows a breath held too long or the suddenness of cold hands touching naked skin. And then the pummeling: like a box of books shaken and slammed down in frustration. Esther's arms had pushed, struck, and seized. They could do little more than drop and hang; she was out of breath. Still, Oyin did not cry. She'd gasped just once at the start. Then, the fight of my mother's arms.

It is said that African mothers never apologize to their children. I would have believed this, too, had I not heard my mother's apology later that night. Esther came into our bedroom. She might have thought we were asleep, or it just didn't matter. She sat at the bottom edge of our bed and bent forward at Oyin's feet. "I'm very sorry," she whispered into the dark. In their shakiness, those words must have come at the end of crying.

Why had my mother fought Oyin so hard? The effort we make to be kindly perceived by kin or stranger is a battle that is evergreen. To be good and respectable, privately, is not enough—the world must think so too. In Oyin's case, a girl who put her own pleasure above modesty taunted the legacy of tradition.

A light from outside our window settled on Oyin's face as she shifted under the sheets. Her lashes flickered, and I saw that they were wet. I lay there thinking I wanted out of it all, the constraints of our culture. I wondered if Oyin, too, felt that way.

OYIN COMING TO LIVE with us was a marked protrusion in the terrain of my childhood. She was my sister; I'd known this without ever being told. Awareness of her preceded any other memory. But we were close in the only way that children of the same father, different mothers, were allowed to be: cautiously familiar. Striving to retain the patriarch's affections undergirded everything. Oyin was that other little girl in the inscrutable universe that was my father.

But then her world fell apart. Temi died in her sleep. The shock of it—that this could happen to someone so young and healthy—meant that spiritual warfare had been waged and she had lost. Her family wanted nothing to do with the darkness that claimed her. Oyin, being Temi's daughter, was something tangible they could rebuke—this is what we heard. So she was sent to live with my father and his latest wife.

Two months later, in our parlor, Sani and Esther sat across from each other for the first time in years, since we fled Elekuro. All of Oyin's belongings sat in two plump leather bags beside her. Face resting in hands, elbows resting on knees, her thighs pressed together and swaying—sloughing away the minutes between then and her future.

"That, you don't have to worry about." My father massaged the arms of the chair and crossed his ankles. He looked down, nodding at the carpet. "I'll send her allowance on the first of every month." My mother looked past him, every part of her stone-still. Sani turned to me and winked. "It will be good for you girls to live together."

That night, after Sani left, after I'd helped Oyin take her bags to my room, I lay in our bed and listened. Somebody always walked home. Somewhere between my window and their destination, another someone wished them well or a good night. Oyin slept on her side and combed the walls with her fingers, as if tracing dreams. Her scapula, stretched through skin, angled through my old nightgown.

"Well, you have to share some things now because your sister has little left to her name, isn't that right?" Esther had said. Years ago, Temi stole what had belonged to her. Now Oyin, like a beggar, had to pick through my worn-out clothes. My mother's triumph was complete.

⌒

EXACTLY ONE WEEK AFTER I turned sixteen, Esther drove onto There but for the Grace in the Beetle. Nearly all the street's residents gathered to watch, some even unlatching their babies mid-suckling, hoping to catch a glimpse. My mother, having missed the dream of earning a university degree, had instead, like her mother, opened a well-loved restaurant. Esther's Palace made Ibadan proud, selling only traditional Yoruba dishes like amala and gbegiri and efo riro. Anything that had been diluted by English influence or adapted from other ethnic groups' cuisines wasn't permitted on the menu. And still, she was a "nonentity food-seller woman," the gossips said. So, the next morning, questions arose and then spread through the neighborhood about how Esther might have come upon the car:

"Ah ah, abi she is the only one in the neighborhood to work hard?" it was asked.

"No," it was decided. "Just as many people, if not more, worked as hard as Esther."

"What about those of us with a university degree? We haven't bought a new car."

"Weeell, she never completed a degree. But even if she did, that doesn't entitle her to a car. A decent restaurant? Yes, we'll give her that." The origins of this car, they then said, must be ascertained.

"Who has she slept with to get this car?" it was asked.

"Ehn hehn, now that is the question that needs asking. Which one of these riffraff returned her sexual favors by way of a car?"

"Now we're talking!" The matter was settled, for then.

⌒

NIYI WAS A SYNTHESIZER: a person who, in truth, did not say anything new or groundbreaking, but whom you'd come to think was brilliant, nonetheless, because he could recite the most interesting part of everything he'd read or heard. And because he added these tidbits at the most pertinent moments in random conversations, and in ways that you never could—in ways you'd never think to—you thought he was always on the cusp of discovery. "My god, he knows it all," you'd say with pride, because you knew him.

By the time I reached senior secondary school, I could name which neighborhood girls Niyi had been with, and which, in their scorn, would attest, if asked, to his rather unremarkable penis. "A stunningly handsome man, a stunningly small penis," one had said.

"You know, I have cousins and cousins overseas," Niyi bragged to me, one afternoon in the back of his car.

"Oh, I see." I looked out the window, away from his waiting. At the front tires of his Daewoo, a toddler pulled a stringed train through the dirt.

Niyi looked at me, slightly turned lips hovering laughter or derision—a mastered ambivalence. A man who mentioned relatives abroad wanted you to press him for more. And if you lacked discretion, you might tell him you wanted the same for yourself.

"I'm not one of those girls whose only dream in life is to go overseas, you know." I sucked my teeth to feign casualness that wasn't down deep. I'd already begun to desire it: someone who could make me an easier life—a ticket to America or something grand like that. Some girls had it that way without even trying—why not me?

"All right, okay, you're not. Are you better than the rest?" Niyi asked exaggeratedly, as men do, to take a woman down a notch for believing in herself.

"No, no—" The pitch of my voice hinted at defensiveness I'd have denied. "I don't think I'm better. America would be great, of course. I just want more than that."

"More, like what?" Niyi sat up and tapped the tip of his cigar into the metal ashtray on the console. He opened the door and pushed spit through the side of his teeth; I wiped the back spray from my cheek.

"I don't know," I said. "A university degree, a life of my own?" Thinking now on those days with Niyi, this is the moment I can't forget. The uncertainty—the question mark—of what it meant to have a life of my own.

"So what, you can't have that in America?" Had I been naive, I would have believed him: that in that simple asking, he had some good, secret plan for me.

"Of course I can. But I want it here. I mean, what if America never comes?" I straightened myself between his legs. "What happens to the girls whose dreams don't come true?"

An aunty of mine had spent a year in America, and it wasn't at all what she'd dreamed. The streets were full of trash, she'd told me and Esther, and there were no movie stars to be found. At our markets, though, the women who had been blessed with time abroad still made the journey seem desirable. It wasn't the clothes they wore or the designer bags they carried. There was an ease in their foreheads, a softness in their eyes, an absence of worry that said life hadn't been just a series of obstacles to survival. But for then, school, Oyin, and life on There but for the Grace would have to do. I still preferred the lull of rainy mornings and the safeness of daily monotony.

⌒

I HELD ON TO Niyi, if only in thought, because my mother's nose was much too keen for anything else. But soon—because thoughts alone aren't enough for long, and because they can run amok in the face of nothing else to do—my thoughts turned to feelings, and my feelings became longing on the days Esther worked late into the night. Niyi would drive by in his blue Daewoo, s-l-o-w-l-y enough that I couldn't miss him as I waited by the parlor window.

Though there was the possibility Niyi could lead to life abroad, it was also perhaps true that I, like Oyin, just became careless. I, too, had succumbed to the butterflies. The squeeze: that insistent kneading of broad hands. The sigh that follows. The hope of what might come next. Lying in the back seat of his car for the third time, my legs wrapped around his neck, his cross chain dangling between my thighs, Niyi was everything I needed.

"As smart as you are, and you know I think you're damn smart, Amina—" He stopped, took a long drag of his cigar. His eyes narrowed, then reddened, as if he'd inhaled the smoke directly into them. He blew it out. "—a university degree won't get you beyond the belt buckle of a rich man's trousers. You'll do much better with me taking care of you."

Like those who didn't know how to stoke their dreams absent the premature opinions of others, I told Niyi the one thing I feared might never happen: leaving my mother's house to have my own place far away from There but for the Grace. In a town that only came to me at night, I would walk down an old, wide street with cobblestones and towering trees whose leaves brushed above, branches sparkling with beads of green, purple, and gold.

"Niyi, I'm going to be free," I said. The *free* hung low in my belly. "Close your eyes." He did, and I placed my hand over the lids. "Can you see me walking?" I wanted him to be with me in my dreaming. A purse in the colors of the Nigerian flag slung across my chest. I could reach for dollar bills whenever I wanted, buy whatever I needed. The brightness of the day cut across my face, and I felt full of everything I might someday become.

"I don't see anything but black." He wanted to be—and would be, he said—the only man allowed to pin me down in the back of a car, with my legs around his neck.

"Yes," I agreed. Yes. And then.

⌣

THREE DAYS LATER, I found Niyi's cross chain wedged in the seat crease of my mother's Beetle. The necklace was so much a part of him, he hadn't removed it even when we were entangled in the back seat of his car. I pulled at the cross, and the rest of the chain slid out of the fold; it zipped against the corduroy cloth of the car seat in a short, whiny ditty. I flipped it over for the INRI that would normally be inscribed on its face. There, instead: *Esther Love Niyi.*

The feeling that comes when one has been wounded by a person to whom too much trust has been given too soon comes only once in a blue moon, my mother had said. And if the eyes, the sudden turn of the lips don't give it away, the rest of the body will. A wiry sting will begin in the ears, spiral through the throat, and then seize the chest, where it will poke and prick the ache already there. I held the cross to my lips and wept—not because Niyi had slept with Esther, but because my mother perhaps hadn't bought the Beetle on her own after all. I wondered when Niyi and Esther could have formed the bond of *love*—a word I'd never heard her say. But there it was: evidence that even in my presence, my mother could build a life that didn't include me. I knew then what I would never be: molded by communal gossip and the reach of a man's whims. In our culture, we accepted both as destiny. "Let them say" or "What can you do?" we might respond. But there had to be more to this life for girls like me. Something unnameable, in waking or dream, had told me so. And I believed it somehow, though I did not know yet how it would happen. America would lead me there.

⁓

I WOKE OYIN AT 2:00 AM. Tapped her lightly because I knew she wasn't asleep. The previous night, after I'd told her what happened with Niyi and Esther, she quickly wiped my tears with her shirtsleeve and asked what I wanted to do about it. Before bed, we hatched our plan. Now she waited for me. We knotted our nightdresses to the side, loosely, so we could easily unravel them and slip back into bed when we returned. We threw on some slacks and headed toward the kitchen. My mother coughed; her mattress creaked. We tiptoed back to our room and waited by the door. When she began snoring, I grabbed two plastic buckets from under the kitchen sink and ran to the back of the flat for the shovel. We walked through the alleyway, a scattered patchwork of weeds and rocks that ended at a cement structure that was the communal latrine— all of this took two minutes, if that. My sister and I went one at a time, from the Beetle through the alley to the outhouse and back. We made five rounds each; enough to cover the roof and seats of the car. We were back in bed shortly after 4:00 AM, just as it began to rain.

ESTHER COULD NOT LET it go. She needed to know who would do this—pour feces on her new car. Even days later, the neighbors—otherwise adept at manufacturing and distributing gossip—remained silent, as if they couldn't smell what came from next door. In a place where nothing was ever really a secret, because There but for the Grace was as much the residential maxim as the street name, it was odd, my mother said, that no one had seen or heard a thing. "Not even the tiptoeing of men going to and from the outhouse? I know it had to be one of these useless men. They can't stand a woman doing well. Especially one doing better than them!"

Who were these people with the gall, the restraint to keep from vomiting in the face of excrement that had sat for so long? Her questions quickened with her pacing. Back and forth, back and forth, between the kitchen and parlor. On a single sheet of paper, one by one, she listed the potential perpetrators: anyone who had not been happy for her and did little to hide it; anyone who had not been happy for her and hid it quite well—someone who had smiled when they met her in the supermarket, but whose joy was only skin-deep. Perhaps even one of the women gathered at the roadside on the day she drove up in the Beetle.

"Maybe it was Madame Lawal," I said. "You remember what she whispered to the supermarket cashier." It was said that Madame Lawal was the first to inquire whom my mother had slept with to get the Beetle. She had asked with such sourness, her lips twisted up in the same way they had when she referred to my mother as that "nonentity food-seller woman."

"Ehn hehn!" Esther nodded. She liked the idea—that Madame Lawal was the saboteur—because Madame Lawal had the arrogance to badmouth my mother for years and yet still eat at Esther's Palace every Tuesday afternoon. She ordered the same dish each time, and sat at the same table. Almost always with a new suitor. Esther resented her, but Madame Lawal was a paying customer, so she held her peace.

⁓

THIS TUESDAY, THOUGH, my mother waited for Madame Lawal, eyeing her table from behind the kitchen counter. She wouldn't serve Madame Lawal herself, not when the entire room could see. Instead, she sent a junior waitress; if matters unraveled, at least the suspicion would begin there. Exactly what Esther put in Madame Lawal's food, she'd never say. But Oyin and I suspected poisoning when she quietly waved the chef aside and insisted on making Madame Lawal's lunch herself.

Talk of Madame Lawal's subsequent illness made the late-night rounds. After returning home that evening, it was said, Madame Lawal dismissed her suitor and washed up for bed. Then she let out a scream so loud—so unlike the usual ones she released when a suitor visited—the street reporters were obliged to rush onto the scene.

Madame Lawal's vomiting spell, it was agreed, was the result of poisoning:

"Who hates this woman?" it was asked.

"It must be someone she has wronged. Someone who doesn't want it to go well for her."

"Well, who has she not wronged? Who is it that actually wishes the woman well?"

"Let us forget that part. Where was she last, before that god-awful scream?"

"Esther's restaurant. It was Esther," they concluded.

"Of course! She's jealous of Madame Lawal's prowess."

There, the matter was resolved.

Aside from this talk, there was no proof of what had happened. And for all its angst, There but for the Grace was not a place where suspicion alone warranted confrontation. Such things were just not done. On a street whose name was biblically inspired, a kind of moral code prevailed. My mother knew this. So did I and Oyin; our silence was secured.

Madame Lawal remained in bed for weeks with a stomach tear, the unintended effect of what "should have only caused a few nights of diarrhea," Esther insisted. "I wanted her to lose a few clients, that was it."

"Who will court her now?" the neighborhood asked.

"Sad, really."

⌒

I NEVER DID ASK Esther about Niyi. I didn't have room, inside the shame. And not knowing was a kind of comfort.

The next time Niyi drove his Daewoo by our flat, he didn't slow down in front of the parlor window. I'd waited each evening since finding the cross chain, wondering whether he would come. I didn't know if I would get in, but I'd wanted the choice. Not that day. Two flats over, a girl maybe a year or two older than I nearly fell out of her blouse running through her yard to his car. This time there was no ringing in my ears, no achy chest. Maybe a small lurch in the gut—the kind that comes with seeing something a bit unexpected, or with the fading of hope I didn't know I still held. But nothing remarkable, like the butterflies or the sigh at insistent hands. The feeling came and went with little fanfare; subdued, nothing to prove.

I walked out of my flat, out of the gate, and onto the road. Already in my nightdress and barefoot too, I imagined the street would soon have a story to tell about me looking this way— one that would make the rounds by sundown. They might say I was just like Esther: wild and a little crazy. Careless about appearances.

A warm mix of rocks and earth settled under my feet. At the corner where There but for the Grace met Elekuro sat an aging rock; it marked where the latter became the former, and where, as soon as one saw it, she knew she was about home. A weathered greenish brown, it had been there longer than the streets themselves. I sat on that rock and waited—for nothing more or less than eternity.

Part II

*Iyanifa, Mother
of Mysteries*

IYANIFA: LAILA

Shells in the shape of women

I CAN TELL YOU THAT ONE OF THE SOULS RETURNS HERE, to the rock in the town of her foremothers, sixteen years after the storm. The shells tell me so.

⌒

AT THE CENTER OF the roundabout, there it sat, bottom hemmed in by overgrown grass and needly weeds. Apata Ayeraye—Eternal Rock—was a greenish-brown mound, tall and broad in the middle of the circle where the fabled There but for the Grace of God Go I Avenue met Elekuro Street and two other roads.

The rock had been there since the founding of the town, the beginning of the Yoruba. The formation, one of the oldest on earth according to those who studied such things, rested unencumbered by all that went on around it.

The town's people, animals—stray and led—and various things with wheels rarely waited their turn at the roundabout; all at once, they'd fly into the tumult, unconcerned. Market women matched the earliness of dawn, walking the edges of the circle with their errand girls lugging merchandise behind them. Office workers hurried to the food stands during too-short lunch breaks. Taxi drivers showed off their navigation skills, proud at barely missing pedestrians heading home at twilight. Coming out of the circle safely was mostly a matter of luck, though some said it was the rock that protected the ones who acknowledged its power.

Somewhere underneath Eternal Rock is buried the town's very first iyanifa, my foremother, conduit of Orunmila, the Oracle of Knowledge. Her gift to her town when she died was to impart wisdom to those who sought it. Whatever the question, at any time of day, you could sit on the rock to wait for an answer. In the thick of the mayhem that was the roundabout, the truth would arrive as a vision or a voice—words filling the air.

But even in death, my foremother was selective: not everyone who came to the rock received an answer. Maybe it was the side on which the querent sat, or the article of clothing worn. Or perhaps it was the depth of desperation displayed. Head-shaking, talking to oneself aloud, or agitated hair pulling might have furthered one's case. Olodu knows.

Laila, nineteen years old, a fledgling artist full of searching, knew the question she had in mind; she'd held it all these years. But whether the Oracle would answer was a different matter. Laila turned from the car window to the man beside her.

"*Okuta?*" This was the word she'd mostly heard used.

He smiled at her intonation. Despite his time in the US, it still amused him how hard Americans tried.

"The Yoruba word for rock," he said.

"And *apata?*" She'd heard this used too.

"Also the Yoruba word for rock. But the word you use depends on the size and magnitude of the rock itself. *Okuta* for a small rock, like a stone, one that can fit here." He used his palm to demonstrate. "*Apata* for a massive one, like the one you will see."

Laila was grateful for his presence. Despite his old age, he'd driven for days, showing her the various streets, expertly handling the police roadblocks and paying the right amount for bribes. He shared the things he knew easily and was warm in a way meant to put her at ease. She was happy to have him there. But there was more she wanted to know. It was the two women—sitting in the back seat—who had the answers.

On behalf of the women, I have sought the Oracle. Before Orunmila speaks, though, let us trace how Laila, the man, and the two women arrived here.

IYANIFA: AMINA AND ESTHER

Shells in the shape of themselves

THERE IS AMINA'S STORY; THERE IS ESTHER'S STORY. There are the stories they tell themselves. And then there's the truth—I tell you of it.

⁓

ESTHER RAN WORDS IN a round until her voice rasped. Tired, her hands held the back of her hips. She had given up so much. Now, on her daughter's nineteenth birthday, she needed to know: "Amina, what do you want to do with your life?"

"With my whole life?" Amina pulled on her braids. "I don't know. Anything—away from here."

For Esther, the uncertainty was enough to end the discussion. She put her hands to her ears and could not bear to hear the rest. Whatever Amina might have meant, Esther had never had the ease of not knowing what came next. For that, she scorned her daughter's simplemindedness.

Still, a mother is expected to unearth what destiny holds for her child. So, when she heard that the traveling prophet was coming again to There but for the Grace, Esther picked through her weekend handbag and the inside pockets of her work brassiere, gathering up whatever she could. Business at the restaurant had been slow since the poisoning of Madame Lawal. She understood that the amount she'd collected was a shameful offering for the request of a prophetic utterance. And that was why she'd stuff the offering envelope with two, three sheets of toilet roll, along with the couple of bills she'd found in her scavenge.

⌒

FIVE DAYS BEFORE the traveling prophet's arrival, Esther rehearsed her earnest face and the angle at which she would bow her head to feign worry. Relying on her clout as a business-woman, too, she went to Amina's boss-lady at Gbagi Market and insisted to the woman's dubious smirk that her daughter was knocked out with something like malaria—she didn't know, she couldn't tell. "It's hard to say with these things, but I would estimate she will need five more days of rest. At least."

Esther and a reluctant Amina used these five days to pre-pare. They'd already begun to fast, resisting the lure of leftover jollof rice all day. At the hush of the street, not long after the alley dogs had given up for the night, mother and daughter went into their yard, where darkness floated down in layers. Sparks of moonlight ran through tree leaves and across their skin. They spun around and around, each washing down the other's back with sugar and palm oil. They wiped polish from their toenails, filed down the cracks at their heels. After they had decreed and declared in the spirit and rebuked all foul entities, at dawn they laid aside two long white dresses for each of the four days to go.

⌒

ESTHER PULLED A THIN roll of bills from her brassiere. "Admit two, please," she said with the ease of someone who did not need to count. Through the congestion of ailments the church congregants had lugged in, mother and daughter made their way. At each utterance of the prophet's tongue, someone leapt up and raced around the auditorium—this, evidence they had been set free. Scripture by scripture, the prophet preached the crowd into all manner of expectation: a new car, canceled debts, prodigal sons and daughters returning home contrite. The air was damp and salty with hope.

Despite what these so-called prophets want us to believe, a good life is more than ease. Ifa demands a reshaping of character. It asks us to shed all that keeps us from becoming who Olodu created us to be. Nothing is wrong with faith, of course not. But faith that does not lead to new deeds is useless.

In any case, Amina and Esther pushed through the others to get into the prophet's line of sight. That the weight of his palm might rest on their heads; that he might speak to them a word that would come to pass. "Yaaaow!" The woman whose foot Amina stabbed with the heel of her sandal pulled and held her dress as ransom for the offense. But Esther, less than a pace behind, mean-eyed the woman into the floor. And the woman—willing to be ruthless anywhere but here—looked away, sorry to have been provoked. She'd come for her daughter's polio-induced limp. At the thought of her child, she patted her dress pocket to be sure the money was still there. They were all here for a prophecy, after all.

Amina stood at the bottom of the stage. She mouthed words into her hands, hoping this humble display of piety might evoke pity and move the prophet her way. And though she questioned whether these things even worked, she waited and prayed. The prophet, hijacked by the tide of the spirit, began slapping everyone who neared the back of his hands. His leaps, erratic and farther away now, made Amina doubt he'd ever reach her at all.

And then the man next to her collapsed. "The spirit's got him!" someone shouted. But it was also hot, and the man, a builder, had been on his feet all day with as little room to breathe then as now. He stumbled to the floor, and the feet surrounding him slid to the side like a dance, giving him the clearance he needed for his prostration before god.

Then just like that, the prophet's hand was upon Amina's head, and he began to speak. "It's because you're husbandless," he said. This was the root of her angst. But fortunately for Amina, he had a specific word from god: before the end of that very year, she would meet her husband. "He'll take care of love and life." Esther put her arms around Amina, ready to walk away, when the prophet continued: "If marriage doesn't happen this year, death might follow the next."

Esther and Amina turned to each other, mouths agape. Could this really be true?

With the encouragement of ushers flanking the prophet, Esther threw the padded envelope into the basket at his feet. He looked at it and scratched the side of his head. "Weeell, it's a kind of death so to speak. You understand? These things are not always so literal. But death is death, why parse words?"

"But how will we know it's him?" Esther needed to be sure. She was amazed by this revelation from the prophet, without his being told that Amina was yet to marry—this was the power of god at work.

"His name will mean *promised land*," the prophet yelled back. He'd already leapt a yard away.

Some women who had overheard all this—Amina's prophecy of love and life—curled their lips. One gave her hair and nails the dirty once-over. Waiting for something to come, too, the women had become cruel. Amina kept her eyes on the prophet and her hands inside her mother's. They held on to each other and the hope of the months ahead.

⌒

NOW, TIMES WERE GRAVE. Amina's prophecy was to have manifested by the end of the previous year. She was nearing twenty-one, and still nothing had come. Esther and her two girls lived day in and out on There but for the Grace, little of note materializing. Though Esther had begun to claim Oyin as a second daughter, if she were fully honest, it was Amina, the child of her womb, whose future she worried about. That was why she had not bothered taking Oyin along to the prophet's visit.

Amina's eyes, Esther thought, were becoming like dundun drums: long and hollow. But inside them hung the echoes of a different disappointment. Amina, hardly concerned with a husband, longed for a path wholly new and hers alone.

A call to recover Amina's destiny; that was how Esther interpreted the flickering gray and black that dashed through her nightly sleep. In one vision, she'd seen Amina holding a pack of dirty diapers. She was sure that someone had declared a season of torment upon her daughter.

"I mean"—Esther tapped the itch underneath her wig—"how can she be satisfied, single and unsettled?" When they were alone at the restaurant, she sought Oyin's advice.

"Mummy, I already told you, you have to let Amina live." Oyin shrugged her shoulders high, hoping Esther would take the hint she didn't want any part of this.

"Let her live? Oyin, what nonsense are you talking? What kind of life can a girl like Amina have without a man to help her along?"

"Have you considered maybe she doesn't actually want a husband? You do realize a woman can be happy without a man, right?"

"Okay"—Esther nodded insincerely—"tell me about one woman you know, in her thirties or even older, who is living happily without a husband?"

Oyin couldn't think of one right then. Not even Esther herself, apparently—it was as if her freedom from Sani now meant nothing at all. But she, Oyin, planned to become one— the very type of husbandless and happy woman about whom Esther had scoffed.

⁓

ESTHER PACED BETWEEN HER and Amina's longing; their desires clashed. She pushed each question up like a rock and dug beneath the decay for an answer. At the urging of her pastor, she went without solid food for days, and trekked into the village mountains where churchless prophets and prophetesses auditioned their gifts for generous offerings. Her dreams persisted.

Amina, too, had a repeating dream. In the middle of some nighttime, she lifted off the ground. And then she flew. Over waving waters, in a forest, weaving through leafless trees. Years later, sitting on a stool in a market stall, looking at her dangling feet, she would remember this dream. She'd stand up and tell herself to levitate. In sleep it had felt so real. Even then, at that stall, she would believe it had happened—that she'd really flown. But there her feet were, heavy and firm on the cobbled ground, nowhere else to go.

Esther was loath to admit that Amina's singleness embarrassed her. She preferred to believe that her own triumphs over men—over Sani, in particular—had liberated her from those kinds of thoughts. Amina wasn't much beyond twenty.

Perhaps it's that she was pretty; more so than Esther, more so than Esther's mother. A new and uncharacteristic quality had emerged in their matrilineal line—there was more to utilize than they'd had before. That Amina was lovely, she thought, broadcasted her singleness as a malady. Something had to be wrong with her. And that meant something was wrong with Esther too.

Amina also felt it, the starkness of going it alone. After secondary school, everyone seemed to walk the world with a destined other. Singleness taunted her beauty. *Why bother?* it might have asked. So Amina stopped wearing face powder. She forsook the straightening comb. Soon the edges of her hair retreated upon themselves like defeat. But there was another thought unfolding: *Anything—away from here.* Her dream had been in a place she was yet to touch. *Promised land* is what the prophet had said.

Esther had a final dream. At the edge of a lake, she sat, facing Amina. A book rested between them. On its cover, a large, hand-shaped bowl emptied its water into a bottomless cup. Amina picked up the book and flicked the pages until the last, from which she read: "Restoration in the land comes after being buried." It was "restoration in the land" upon which Esther seized, ignoring "buried" altogether.

Thus it was that in this new year, rather than return to get a confirming word from the traveling prophet, Esther went simply to give thanks. She danced all the way across the auditorium and threw another padded envelope into the money tray. Love, the arrival of a husband, would soon be a sure thing. Life was everything to follow.

If Esther was consumed by all things marriage, Amina battled her own frightening thoughts. Her boss-lady at Gbagi had not run out of ways to mention her worthlessness. Nothing about Amina, she said, was deserving of the luxurious booth at which they worked selling and sewing ankara, lace, and damask fabrics. Amina was a simple girl, the boss added; this stall was anything but, with its ornamental wallpaper and a designated area by the entrance where clients could pour themselves tea with milk. Still, Amina went to work early and returned home late—each week, saving her earnings. On her one day off, she thought of Niyi and rubbed herself in the draped dark of her bedroom. She remembered this pleasure with him, endlessly more rewarding than the prospect of a husband.

⌒

ESTHER'S CELEBRATORY POSTURE WANED when, still, no husband arrived. Months on, not even the hopeful dream she'd had came true. And she could see it, Amina's thinning body— bottom pushed out from a dwindling waist. In that silhouette, Esther found a kind of relief. "Coca-Cola bottle! At least you still have your figure, thank god." She flicked her daughter's breasts.

Amina rolled her eyes and pushed Esther's fingers away. She toyed with insolence; it was an abomination to hit one's mother.

"But a little face powder wouldn't harm you." Esther rubbed the edges of Amina's hair. Even there, nothing new had sprung. "And I have a straightening comb you can borrow."

For the first time since childhood, Amina met her mother's eyes. "Husband or not, I will be happy."

"Happy?" Esther wrung her hands. Amina must have forgotten that *happy* in English has no meaning in Yoruba that is separate of marriage. "Abi what will they say, Amina?"

⌒

FINALLY. ESTHER REMEMBERED THAT a friend of a friend—
because no friend would admit it personally—knew an Ifa
priestess that had dedicated herself to the service of women.
Esther had known other iyanifas before, through her mother
and in the river city. But this iyanifa, it was said, believed her
powers, as endowed by Orunmila, rivaled and exceeded those
of any babalawo or other iyanifa in Yorubaland. Women as far
away as Benin and Togo sought her counsel. "The woman is
the kernel of the earth. No man can tell her story," the priestess
was believed to have said.

I am that Ifa priestess—the mother of mysteries whose
knowing is unmatched, even among the men. Like most, I
was born into this religion, into a family of Ifa adherents.
My father was the assigned aborisha for our family's clan,
taking to the shrine the required offerings. I went with him
to worship because I was his only child; had he a son, I know
the story would be different. That is why I believe my work
is destiny—Olodu ensured that the role of diviner would be
mine. Long before Esther came into this life, I knew the day
of our meeting. How does one welcome a stranger that is
already known?

⌒

NEXT TO MY HOUSE is a plain, portable storefront. There,
toiletries, snacks, and all manner of knickknacks are sold.
Many customers come and go without a clue of the store's true
purpose. Seekers of the Oracle must visit there first, prepared
for the steps that will lead them to me. Most who need me
find me through the word of others, inquiring about my work
beforehand and receiving instructions on what to do when
they arrive. First, the querent will ask to buy a bar of herbal
soap. The shopgirl, who is also my daughter, then takes the

money for the soap along with the amount corresponding to the complexity of the answers sought.

Though many desperately seek an answer from Orunmila, few will heed his guidance. In Ifa, shifting the direction of one's life depends on this: accepting the divine assessment of the root cause of an issue, and then following the prescribed steps. The seeker may be asked to offer a sacrifice to remedy their suffering. It is Ifa that determines what the querent must do. The specific odu, the sacred wisdom of the 256 verses in the holy book, is drawn out by the outlay of the merindinlogun—sixteen—shells.

WHEN I AM READY to divine, the cowrie shells—owo eyo—are loosely constellated on a wooden plate. The querent and her mother sit side by side, pressed together, legs folded behind them. Daughter's fingers pinch the money to her lips. She must not speak aloud; in silence, she tells Orunmila the problem for which she is ready to have an answer. I will depend on the shells alone, my spirit communing with the Oracle to hear the question and offer the correct solution. I begin to praise-chant Orunmila—drawing out his essence, power, and beneficence from the beginning of time to the moment at hand. The cowrie shells, sixteen in all, you remember, are thrown onto the wooden opon ifa and they land where they might. I am quiet, hearing all that is said and unsaid, seeing all that is seen and unseen. Ase! An answer for the daughter comes forth.

But in this instance, the mother did not bring her daughter. Esther came to me alone. On the straw mat, money to mouth, in silence, she asked: "When will Amina get married?"

I threw the shells, and all but four landed within the wooden tray.

"Nothing of this is about marriage," I said.

"What do you mean?" Esther asked. For mothers in this culture, everything is about marriage. How else do women survive men?

The answer had been given as eewo—I said—the one thing Amina must never do because it is taboo.

"Well, what is it?"

I pulled Esther's head close, her ear to my mouth, should the opposing spirits be listening. Orunmila had made a declaration. It was certain.

"Is there an offering we can make, something else I can do?" Esther was doubtful, still.

"No."

⌒

OUR CITY IS A small place. My side door is open at all times. Those who pass by wonder of the happenings inside—why, for instance, is my door perpetually open, even at night? I like to hear the world, I say. Nothing is starker than the uncertainty of voices in the night. That evening, I watched Esther walk into the hum of an early dark to begin her journey home.

"What did the shells say?" Amina asked her mother, as soon as she entered their kitchen.

"Well, four fell out of the opon ifa, so—"

"Four days, four months? What does that mean?"

Esther didn't know what to think about what Orunmila had said would happen in four years, let alone how to tell her daughter. She wasn't even sure she believed it. Like many, her desire for traditional religion was complicated by her cherished Christianity. The prophet had said Amina would be married; I had seen something else altogether. For all Esther knew, I was a charlatan looking for someone to deceive—more pronouncements, more money. But it was not my place to convince. The unfoldment of time does the necessary work.

"Four days, four months." Esther's irritation was evident. "What's the difference, Amina? The thing here is to be patient. In time, god will do what the prophet has said."

"The prophet," Amina repeated. When the thing prophesied did not come to pass, believers would say it wasn't god's will after all, despite their prior insistence to the contrary. "Stupid." She sucked her teeth.

Heat stabbed the ends of Esther's skin. She felt faint. It was heavy in her belly, what I had relayed about Amina. Declarations of destiny can cripple dreams. But there was no way to be sure Amina would do what had been cautioned against, she thought.

Amina knew when Esther was done talking, so she let the matter go. What would be would be, despite the predictions of some prophet or priestess. She went to the kitchen window and there it was, written on the side of a bus:

Visa Lottery Open!
Apply Now, Fly Later!

IYANIFA: LAILA

Shells in the shape of roads

I CAN TELL YOU THAT LAILA TRACES THE PAST, TRYING to find the feeling of home. The shells tell me so.

⁓

OF ALL THINGS FROM her childhood, Laila thought about the photo most often: a mini-size bus, back doors open, parked on a side road at the edge of a market. A man, hardly more than a blur in a white shirt, sat in the last row. Maybe he had just boarded or would get off at the next stop. To the side of the bus were several baobab trees flanking a road that curved away from the photo's corner. Then there were the two goats. One stood inside the back of the bus, eyes staring straight into the camera. Outside, the other goat leapt, legs in midair, about to join its friend.

"If you want to travel swiftly and not be noticed, then you go by way of bus," the old man said. He told her that the danfo, which Laila saw in that photo, was a privately owned passenger bus. Typically yellow and run by a focused driver and no-nonsense conductor, it operated mostly within the city limits.

What about the bus her mother rode when she left this town?

"That's a different kind," he said. Although that bus traveled longer distances from town to town, the same sort of characters and shenanigans as were encountered on the danfo could be found there. He should know, he reminded her; he rode such buses for years before he made it to the US. There were three types of people on these buses: the holy roller, looking to recruit converts; the common traveler, visiting relatives or returning home; the escapee, usually a young or middle-aged woman trying to leave behind an old life.

Laila imagined what it must have been like for her mother when she said goodbye to this place. Had she been afraid, alone on the bus? Did she hope to return?

"Why do you think she went by herself?" Laila asked her companion.

"To get away from the things they might say."

AMINA

Shells in the shape of ghosts

I HAD WANTED, AS WITH FAITH, TO BELIEVE SOMETHING other than what I could see. Had my eyes stopped at the end of There but for the Grace—a street paved with much less than gold—I might have thought this was it. Some might say things weren't bad for me in the ways they were for others, and that would have been true. We weren't desperately poor, and I wasn't abused. But even within the calm of my life, I wanted so much more. "Why can't she just be happy?" family once asked. The things they prized hadn't moved me; I took my time feeling for life, like fingers through market silk. I wanted much more.

"What do you mean, she's still single?"

"Ah, you don't say. I thought she had a prophecy."

"Oh, it hasn't come true. That's too bad, hehn?"

The gossipers on There but for the Grace were very sorry for others' misfortune. Their faces said so. But as the bad news was told, they exhaled. So glad it wasn't them, they would—for the sake of pity—pretend not to have already heard these terrible things happening to you. They would let you tell your story again, nodding and flinching as if it was all new. And in some way it was, because, for that moment, they let themselves enjoy your calamities afresh.

When others were talked about, I'd looked away; when it was me, self-deception became impossible. I could no longer bend every which way, trying to dodge what they said.

⌒

THREE YEARS AFTER the sign on the side of the bus, I decided to give the lottery another try. I walked into the café on Modaran Road, doubtful I would find the computers or REAL INTERNET promised on the cardboard sign outside. But there they were, two rows of cushionless metal chairs facing large computers pressed against peeling green walls.

A paper-size poster taped to the back of the room read in bold, centered print:

- **No Food or Drink!**
- **No 419!!**
- **No Naija Prince Email Scams!!**
- **Stop Embarrassing Your Nation!!!**

A serious-looking man—bundled in a sweater too heavy for the warm day—held his head in his palms. He looked about to cry. Whatever the news on his computer screen, it couldn't have been good.

The overhead lights were dimmed. I felt at ease, almost unseen. I found the computer that matched the number eight on the white paper in my hand. The room attendant walked over and opened the form I needed to fill: US Embassy & Consulate in Nigeria, Electronic Diversity Visa Entry Form.

I gave him his tip. We went through the customary motions: him, pretending it was too much; me, insisting that I insisted; him, already putting the money in his pocket before I finished talking.

"After you complete it, you press here and it will print over there by my desk." He pointed behind him, to the cubicle by the entrance. "Then you come and pay, and I will give you your form. Of course, you will have to submit it at the embassy."

"Of course." I smiled to acknowledge that I understood.

"So you're going to America?" He nodded wildly, then watched my face as if for something to seize.

"I hope so," I said.

"Yeees! Well, that would make you and a hundred million others, hehn!" The bitterness in his laugh sounded practiced and like it couldn't be helped. He would have replied with those words whatever I'd said.

Fifty-five thousand: the number of annual visa slots available for foreigners from low-immigration countries to enter the US. Each year, as soon as the lottery opened, the news blasted through every medium. By lunchtime the next day, internet cafés were packed with young and middle-aged men hunched over battered keyboards. Whatever happened, failing to obtain a visa couldn't be worse than staying in this place, pining for a new life.

I filled out the form, again. Slowly, this round, as I'd been warned after the last time. "Listen, even a simple, unintentional mistake can result in your disqualification. You won't be selected and that's that," the visa agent had said.

Age: 24.
Country of Birth: Nigeria.
Education: Secondary Certificate.

And so on. I hoped my boss at the fabric shop would attest to my six years of training and apprenticeship as a seamstress. That, too, was required.

THE BUS RIDE HOME from the internet café was strange in its newness. I expected the driver to turn onto There but for the Grace, as if I'd forgotten I hadn't lived there in over a year. Just three streets away, on Idunu Lane, my new flat with Oyin was a world of memories removed.

I hid the application in a leather portmanteau that once belonged to my father. By the time I reached home, the steps between the lottery and feet in America seemed spread out beyond impossibility, but I wanted to be ready, in case I was chosen. My own life was on the verge, finally. And I needed help that wasn't Esther's.

I had not seen my father in years, not since the day he'd left Oyin and her bags in our parlor. I'd heard rumors that he had another successful business now—car detailing, they believed. At forty-something, he was still handsome; his belly wasn't yet rounded like the rest of the men his age. And they said, "Good for that Sani. Do you remember when he had to sell cloth at the market, just to get by? Life can turn around in a blink, god bless him!"

"AMINA, YOU'RE SUCH a strange girl! Of course I'll give it to you, why wouldn't I? But be careful, his new wife might not appreciate you calling, you know, with your history." Oyin flipped through her phone diary for Sani's number.

"What history? That was so long ago. As far as I'm concerned, she's no longer my business."

Sani's first wife after Esther, Lara, left him for her pastor. Mary, his new wife, had been my good friend in secondary school. And then I heard she was dating my father. I thought it was just the wild spinning of the gossip wheel, until Oyin's friend saw them holding hands at a play. Behind his back, Mary boastfully referred to herself as "Sani's finest sugar baby," it was said.

Oyin had laughed when I told her the news of Sani and Mary. "Let them live their life, Amina, we're not children anymore. If you have a problem with it, confront them. And if you won't do that, then move on!"

She was so flippant about the affair, I'd asked whether she knew about it before I did.

"What the hell do you mean? You're always thinking someone is out to get you, Amina. Just because I'm not bitter doesn't mean I'm in cahoots to keep things from you." Oyin's implication that I was bitter had stung. And despite her denial, a residue of distrust remained between us.

"Truly, I don't care anymore about Daddy and Mary." I shook my head for added credence.

"If you say so." Oyin offered her pitying frown. "His number hasn't changed all these years, you know." She tapped the page lightly, letting me admire her glittery wine-red nails. I hadn't seen her natural fingers in months. "There, you can write it down."

I put the number in my purse. "Your nails are beautiful, Oyin," I said, trying to deflect notice from my bitten, stubby ones, and from the unsettling talk about Mary.

"I know! I went to the shop, but they didn't know what the hell they were doing. So I opened the girl's tools, took everything I needed, and did the manicure myself. Can you believe it? I swear, it looks better than she would have managed."

I could in fact believe it. While I left my future to chance, Oyin went directly to what she wanted and fearlessly bent it to her will. She spread both hands in front of her face, nails toward me, so I could admire them again.

"Sooo, what are you going to say to Mr. Sani?" Oyin pressed her palms on the edge of the bed and crossed her legs—poised for scandal.

I wouldn't tell her my plans yet. At the restaurant, there'd begun a hushed chattering whenever I walked into a room where Oyin and Esther sat. It was a feeling of being discussed behind one's back and smiled at to one's face, for reasons that would never be known. Perhaps they suspected my hope for America.

"Well—" I said. Talking about my father in this way felt uneasy. "—even though all these years have passed, I want to get to know him again." The way Oyin sat and listened, I knew then without her saying so that she must have found out my plans. And what she might say about the lottery, I couldn't yet bear.

"Just don't do anything that will make your mother go crazy." Oyin scanned my face, as if to confirm I wouldn't do such a thing. "You know you can't afford to be disowned. I can, since I don't have a mother anyway. But not you."

A face of perennial cheer made Oyin prettier than she might have been. I rubbed the side of her hair and looked at them again: the eyes, nose, and mouth that stirred my fear of not being loved enough. We both looked like Sani, yet nothing alike.

"You have me," I said. That was true. "And you have our father." That, too, was true—she always had, and seemed to be the only one. How much of Esther did Oyin possess? For a girl who our culture says is illegitimate by birth, after just nine years with my mother, she was secure in a way I was not. She could make anyone love her. "And no, I won't do anything crazy," I said.

⁓

WE AGREED TO MEET in Lagos, Sani and I. For a while, he'd remained in Harvest River, Ibadan, the place of my birth, even after my mother left him for Elekuro. Moving to Lagos, he told our kin, was the final shedding of a time he'd been trying to forget—working, unsuccessfully, to sell to ungrateful women.

In my childhood, I had been like a ghost floating through my father's house. I hoped the years since had enabled his seeing.

"Daddy, it's me," I said, when I finally called.

"Oyin!"

"No. It's me, Amina." I felt even less myself, having to say it.

"Amina. I didn't recognize your voice." Of course he didn't. I was nineteen when we last spoke; fourteen when he brought Oyin with him to There but for the Grace. "How are you?" Then static. "How is your health?"

"Fine, I'm doing fine," I nodded with the words. The formality of his questions underscored the strangeness between us. I couldn't imagine my mother having to ask about my health, as if I were at a doctor's office for the first time.

I took a bus—nearly three hours—to Lagos. Partway there, I'd been rocked to sleep, bouncing through pockmarked roads. Sani was already waiting when I arrived. His car, a newer Peugeot, was distinct in its cleanness at the border of the dusty motor park. Despite the heat and grime, my father wore his white agbada, overflowing with the elegance of Yoruba tradition. It was true what they'd said about his handsomeness for his age.

But then he reached me and I saw it: while he walked, the jerking of his legs had turned the crisp white hem of his pants to a wet, dirty brown. Rather than the customary kneeling at his feet, I reached out my arms, wanting to hold him.

"Don't worry, Mary is at her mother's," Sani said, as the guard unlocked the gate for the Peugeot to enter his compound.

I wasn't worried. America filled more of my thoughts than the humiliation of his indiscretion. We went inside and I washed up. At dusk, over suya and beers, I sat with my father in his courtyard, reimagining the past.

ESTHER

Shells in the shape of dust

AMINA.

During your childhood, what you would someday think of me troubled my thoughts. I asked god if what I imagined of myself—of my efforts—is what you would attest to, years on. I wanted you to be like me, yet walk a separate path. Could that even be? I prayed to see you become who I had hoped to be.

But despite my admonitions and all the ills I prayed against, the tithings and fasts, the prophets and iyanifas, for a time you took the very road I've known well, within the orbit of the world I had created. What could I do?

Then, at twenty-five years old, you came to tell me of your plans to travel overseas, to America. You had vanquished the stagnation that had held you all those years. Many would have died from it—the feeling, you had said, that quiet suffering was all life held in store. But you managed to edge out from under its weight. You wanted more than I ever did.

"America." As soon as you said it, I regretted the things between us yet unsaid. I recalled my meeting with Iyanifa, four years before. And yet my heart felt heavy with hope. You would leave in exactly one month, having kept from us all the planning that led you here. "I didn't want you to worry," you said.

I wish I'd had more time. We knew already, from the family who went before you, how costly those short, shouting phone calls could be. That was why we agreed to write letters. I wish I'd had more time. Even now.

Amina, it is inconsolable, the pain between my breasts. At night, I retreat into the softness of my memories: you at twelve months, the flat of your feet clinging to my belly as I put you down to sleep. In my dreams, for all the years you've been gone, you are never older than one.

"Rashid and Fatima will welcome you with open arms," I assured you.

You asked how I was so certain.

"Because they know the fragility of being far from home. They won't let anything happen to you."

That was the last thing we talked about before you left. And you were in a hurry to go.

At the time you came, the end of harmattan season, a measure of dust had coated the cement ground as we chattered inside. There is a superstition. It belongs to our people alone. Like much in our culture, it is born of the threat of loss. If you are ever to see the traveler again, the lore goes, their shoes will make a discernible print that even the wildest harmattan couldn't scatter—a message to the one staying behind. *As they go, so they shall return.* A minute after you left, I pushed aside the curtains to see what the ground had to say.

One month later, I began these letters.

IYANIFA: SANI AND AMINA

Shells in the shape of a hand

IF I TOLD YOU THAT THE SIXTH, THE ONE WITH THE dragging leg, has been a catalyst to the other souls' reunion, would you believe it? It is around Sani they gather, though their relationship to him has changed over the millennia. In one life, Amina was his sister; in another, his father. Why things happen this way, Olodu knows—his reasons are unsearchable. What is revealed to me, even in its vastness, is but a glimpse of how the world is shaped.

I can tell you, too, that Sani is the most stubborn of the souls. The ending for him shall be the same as in the past. The shells tell me so.

⁓

SANI'S ENTIRE LIFE HAS hinged on one thing: his inability, even in the privacy of his mind, to admit he was wrong. That he raped his first wife, Esther, he refused to consider a crime. Without it, he wouldn't have been able to marry her, and their daughter Amina would not have been born. That he later married Amina's friend, despite his daughter's distress, certainly wasn't a crime.

Any time he was confronted about either of those two things—by someone in Esther's family, especially—he waved the words off with a smirk intended to sear ridicule into the accuser. In all the years of getting away with things because he could, Sani walked this world with the comfort of a man who believed he was above human justice. A place in his mind safe from outside consequence: this was where Sani lived.

That was until the one lie—the telling of which, the doubling down on of which, and the shameless repetition of which had the trinal effect of destroying his relationship with Amina, alienating those who had wanted to believe in him, and tormenting his mind with the thought that others now saw him for who he was.

But before the ultimate lie, there was a young Sani. Like most children, he had been adorable and promising. His parents wrapped him in an indulgent love that was unusual for that time. It was easy for them: Sani was stunning and so wise. Three dimples pierced his high cheeks. He said things that were well beyond his years. As with every aged soul, many of his utterings—unremarkable to him—held hints of the worlds he had seen.

With the love of Sani also came a dangerous permissiveness, the sort given to a child whose parents nurse unaddressed guilt. It was Sani's mother, of course, who carried the bulk of it. As she told it, her carelessness had led to the polio infection that left her only child partially paralyzed in his right leg: sharing a spoon with him, not knowing she was infected until later, after her boy was deathly ill. When Sani recovered, his parents were so grateful that, from then on, whatever he wanted, he received.

Whether sweets most children only dreamed of or trips many families couldn't afford, Sani's parents committed to securing for him—through money or might—a life that made him not just equal, but superior to others. But the treats and trips were not the problem; children eventually learn to appreciate material things. Sani's parents filled him with something more insidious: an enduring spirit of entitlement. Whatever he chose to do, he believed he had the right.

At age eleven, when Sani was caught cheating on a school exam, his parents waged battle against his accusers. They went to the school's headmaster and laid out on his desk several pieces of incontrovertible evidence that he had been sleeping with Sani's teacher. "We don't want your wife to find out about this any more than you do." Sani's mother folded her hands in her lap and waited. Her husband twisted a derisive smile and glanced at his wristwatch. If it wasn't for the headmaster's deep hue, the embarrassment that filled his body would have been apparent.

Sani's parents needn't say more, the headmaster assured them. A week later, the teacher quietly resigned and moved to another town. Sani received a solid mark in the class, and nothing was said again about the cheating.

On the issue of his limp: Sani's parents understood the underbelly of the culture. Their child's disability would be a social detriment. It would be more than that, in fact. Some would say it was a curse; others would insist the family had reaped what it sowed in this or a previous life. Bad things happen to bad people, they might proclaim. But I know for certain that no one is all good or wholly evil. Olodu has made us flawed and with a hunger to improve—how we fill this need is up to us.

⌒

WHEN SANI WAS ABOUT TWELVE, when the limp had become his distinct way of moving about in the world, his father drove him to an open field several kilometers from their house. As soon as the car stopped, he opened the passenger's side door and pushed the boy out. Sani fell face-first into the door panel and tumbled to the ground.

"Up, get up and walk. Go!"

Sani began walking the only way he could: uneven and jerky. His father stood, hands on his hips, by the side of the car—disappointment tight in his jaws. Sani stopped walking and turned back. His eyes burned. But he knew better than to cry. "What am I supposed to do?" he yelled back at his father.

"Walk with your dignity, Sani. Stop looking down at that dead leg. What can it do for you, hehn? You walk with your head like this." His father straightened his neck and pushed his shoulders back to show him how.

So that was what Sani did—walk, head up. He saw himself as fully unstoppable, in spite of a leg that begged to differ. He imagined there had never been a limp. He walked with confidence not just matched to the other boys', but notably exceptional.

After that day in the field, everyone still talked about Sani's limp behind his back, though not in the disparaging way his father had warned about. And maybe if Sani had known this— that despite his leg, many spoke of how brave he was—he might have been less inclined toward the contempt he felt for them all.

Contrary to the cultural conjectures, I can tell you that Sani's leg is not a punishment for offense in this or another world. Souls forget that there are things, seen and unseen, we take with us into every life. So it was that in his very first one, thousands of years before, Sani had broken his leg running through rocky ground, trying to save Esther from a donkey that had lost its mind. Theirs is a love and hate that has persisted through the ages. In every incarnation since the first, the weakened leg has reemerged from a different cause—a polio infection, this time.

At an age when many of his mates were obsessed with football and the attention of girls, Sani cultivated an oppressive religiosity within which this sole binary existed: saint/sinner. Everyone was a sinner except for Sani, of course. He lived daily by a book of his own words, reinforced by scripture. If he wrote it down, then he could embody it. His favorite entry: *I won't curse today. Ephesians 4:29 says: "Let no corrupt communication proceed out of your mouth, but that which is good to the use of edifying, that it may minister grace unto the hearers." No evil will come from my lips. Amen.*

Sani had become such a man: one whose mouth honored god. Lying, though, was a different and private matter. Ephesians 4:29 was solely about curse words because that was the thing he struggled with outwardly, and which others could easily judge. For the sake of god, he had to be blameless in his speech.

⁓

THIS IS HOW THE lie began.

Amina had called Sani—she might as well have dropped from the sky. Pretending, as he had in recent years, not to have children, *Daddy* felt like a word that had nothing to do with him. When he really thought about it, his distance from Amina had been less about Esther, and more that he enjoyed his new life married to a younger woman who, to his incredible fortune, did not want a child.

Yet when Amina said she needed his help, he couldn't refuse. He hardly knew her now, given how little he had seen the girl since Esther divorced him. But she was his last-born and that still conjured a certain pride—his child needed him.

The question Amina had asked was tremendous: Could he pay half of the plane fare, should the visa lottery come through?

One half of a plane ticket to America was no small thing. Years of saving, going from relative to relative begging to borrow, humiliating oneself, were necessary acts to secure that amount of money. Tales are often told about such efforts, usually by those who command the privilege to make or break the dreams of the needy.

"That's no problem," he had reassured her. It was important that she thought him generous. Esther had said terrible things to the girl about him, he was sure, so his kindness would cast some doubt on her grumblings.

But there was a problem: Sani didn't have the money. No one knew it then, but he was near bankrupt. The cash from his new business paid off debts on the old business. And money from the old business had gotten him out of the hole from those many years ago. A man like him—once a company executive—having to sell cloth at Harvest Market to feed his family was a shame he couldn't repeat. But here he was again, tottering on the edge.

If Sani did not look like a man on the brink, this was deliberate. In our culture, appearance is a weapon of survival—favor is showered upon those who already look blessed. And because grace begets more grace, the fortunate remain so. However long he could help it, Sani would be well-dressed and his car would be the best he could afford. Further debt for the sake of others' respect and even envy was worth the price he paid.

Too much shame and pride—the reasons Sani didn't tell Amina he couldn't afford to help her. "God willing, you will win that visa," he'd said. What he really hoped was that things would not progress far enough for her to need the money. So when Amina was selected for an interview, Sani spun into panic.

He dug into his spare savings and let her borrow the amount she'd asked for, nonetheless. It was an embarrassment to promise one's child a thing and then renege. But now he would have to get it back. His first thought—call Oyin and ask her to find the envelope of cash somewhere in Amina's belongings—was nonsense. Still, he asked her to do it.

"No. Unh unh," she had said. "How could you do that to your own daughter?"

I know that Oyin could have said much more. She could have expressed disappointment that Amina hadn't told her about America in the first place—anger that she found out only because Sani wanted her help stealing. But she wanted to keep her place, outside the triad that was Sani, Esther, and Amina. She would confront her sister when the time came.

As the days passed, the chances of Amina buying the plane ticket increased. And so did Sani's frustration. He decided to visit. He was in Ibadan on business, he told her.

Amina had a half day at the fabric shop, but would be home in the afternoon, she told Sani when he called. Her boss allowed her to leave early on the days when there would be less measuring and sewing to complete, and Amina was not needed to do the work.

Sani sped recklessly to Ibadan, trying to reach the girls' flat while Amina was still at work. Alas, he was too late.

As soon as Sani came inside, Amina felt the burning in her chest. Absent of it her whole life, her father's attention these last few months frightened her. It was a feeling like *this won't last*, and when his caring ended, she would have to return to wondering if he had loved her at all. Sani evoked within Amina a craving that could not be fed. They talked around each other, their minds flittering in and out of elsewhere. Finally, Sani gave her cash to go buy them soft drinks from the corner cart. When Amina left, he thought perhaps he might have his chance.

He walked around his daughters' sitting room, tense and yet amused by all the things—junk and treasure—the two girls had collected in the short time they'd lived together. Amina had become enchanted by wooden animals—goats, in particular—carved and sold by artisans at the markets. On the wall behind the sofa, Oyin curated vintage photos of Yoruba elites living the high life. Sani tried not to be nosy. He fingered the stringed sculpture on the shelf. He wanted to flip through the photo album on the center table but decided against it. He'd learned to avoid what he didn't want to see: pictures of Esther and their old life. On the dining table, Amina had left scatterings of papers and receipts, worthless things that would sit there forever.

And there, as if by divine trickery, was Amina's purse, hanging off a chair's shoulder. In that cursed instant, having no time to debate, Sani pulled the zipper and went straight to the bottom. He felt a thick roll of bills, yanked it out, and shoved the money in his pocket.

He didn't know how much was there, or if it was even the same cash he had given her. His heart beat in his ears. It was already done.

Esther had always been the one Amina turned to, even as a child. It sickened Sani, the way they clung to each other, leaving him cast aside. Still, he'd made peace with living on the periphery of his daughter's life. Despite his moving her out of his home after Temi died, Oyin had been more willing to have a relationship with Sani, and for that alone, he loved her a little bit more—though if asked, of course he would deny it. He took the visits Esther occasionally offered and embraced the birthday wishes from Amina when she remembered. But it gnawed at him: Amina didn't fear him the way he'd had to fear his own father.

Oh, and it didn't matter—not to Esther, and certainly not to the girl—that he thought Amina dressed too loosely. He could hardly believe what she was wearing when he'd picked her up at the motor park. He'd stared at her bare arms, trying to submit her into covering them up. Of course, she didn't. He was comforted remembering how Oyin's skirts swept the ground, modestly.

Amina had shrugged off his disapproval. Esther would roll her eyes. Sani didn't like that at all. And he didn't like that other men could make out the shape of Amina's body in the clothes she wore. If she wasn't his daughter, he would have called her the same well-deserved names he called other girls who dressed like her. Esther had allowed all of this to happen, and he hated her for it.

But because there was nothing Sani could do about any of that, he fantasized about his vindication. He wanted, somehow, to prove to himself that all the bad feelings he'd had toward Esther were justified. And though he hadn't planned or thought through this moment, he relished the control he now had. The amount he took from Amina was quite a lot—it could delay her plans to leave the following month.

And if Sani was honest, it made him sad that Amina hadn't even offered to file for him, her own father. Anyone in her position would have included their parents on the visa form. Her selfishness, though unsurprising, still upset him. For a moment, his legs felt weak and he had to sit down.

He went back to the shelf and picked up a small picture frame: Amina, age five, in a yellow print dress. Sani stood next to her in a plaid suit, arms behind his back. His old white Peugeot 505 filled the space behind them.

"Daddy, what happened to that car?" Amina had walked through the door, their drinks in hand.

"I wrecked it. I think it ended up in alhaji's junkyard." Sani's whole body felt hot. He hadn't heard her coming. He watched her face for a hint of what she might have seen. Nothing.

"I loved that car."

It was the memory of it that Amina loved. That car coming down the road meant a visit, and maybe even gifts from her father. The other memories of the Peugeot were emblematic of her relationship with Sani: when the car was brand new, he'd taken Oyin for a ride in it first. In spite of his words, Amina wondered if it was Oyin Sani had come to see. If asked, the sisters would say they were close. That was why they chose to live together. But if pressed, they'd admit that Sani remained the most difficult silence between them. What he was to one, the other longed for.

Amina was relieved when Sani said he was leaving. She didn't want him to see that she'd begun to shake. When he turned toward the door, she steadied herself on the arm of the sofa. What her father had done—what she'd seen him do, from the window, on her way back into the flat—was ripe for denial. She wanted to be convinced, from thin air maybe, that she hadn't seen Sani take the cash. Coincidence could make its own case: Sani just happened to be by her purse, and the money just somehow disappeared; the former didn't lead to the latter.

The rest of the money she'd saved for her plane ticket to America, in dollars—that was what Sani stole. And he took more than he had let her borrow. She wouldn't let herself believe it. Her future, bright and crisp, had been wrapped up in those bills. Sani had snatched it without pause. Amina had watched him slip the cash casually into his pocket with the unbothered ease of someone who thought he had the right.

⌒

AMINA CONFRONTED SANI. She didn't fear what he might say because he was no longer hers to lose. Later that night, after he had left—in bed, turning through dreaming—she'd decided.

She begged for the day off from the shop and took the bus to Lagos. Sani responded in the ways that had absolved him since he was a child. First, anger: "Ah ah, Amina. Are you serious? You're accusing me of stealing! From you?" That didn't stick, so then calm: "I swear, I didn't do it," he told his daughter, in a breath slightly above a whisper. Nothing in his eyes or voice revealed more than what he'd said. But it was the words themselves. Amina thought they lacked the details one would have offered when telling the truth. It was as if he'd had those words ready, awaiting her accusation. Sani believed that if he declared a thing with enough anger or charm, there was nothing more to say.

"OF COURSE I WANTED to believe him," Amina later told Esther.

Esther worked herself up quickly. It pricked her nerves that she still had to push this point with her daughter. "How can you even say that, Amina? The man is a liar." It was taboo to speak ill of a child's father. Esther did not care.

"I saw him do it. But he's still my father." At least there was that, his title. He'd done so little else for her, helping to pay for a plane ticket wasn't much to ask. "If he wanted the money back, why not just tell me? Or has he lost his mind?"

Esther, versed in all the shades of Sani, knew that he hadn't lost his mind. At least not in the way Amina might have hoped. "His behavior doesn't surprise me at all, at all." She had told Amina so little about her life with Sani, the girl hardly understood her father. "No, my darling, your father hasn't lost anything."

ESTHER SNATCHED HER CHANCE for exoneration. She wanted the world, the one that knew her and Sani, to see him for who he was. For those who were still calling her a witch, all these years later, to be ashamed for having chosen Sani's side. So she'd gone to the pastor of their old church—the place of worship they had shared way back, when they were still married.

"Pastor, come on now, you know she convinced the girl to make this up to destroy my name," Sani responded when confronted. And because he believed it gave weight to his words, he did what he knew to do—quote scripture: "Blessed are ye, when men shall revile you, and persecute you, and shall say all manner of evil against you falsely, for my sake. Matthew 5:11."

Despite Sani's denial and invocation of scripture, the pastor believed the women. Like the thorough man of god he was, he'd prayed for divine revelation before Sani arrived for their meeting. And in the end, Sani laid himself bare.

"Why do you think Amina is running to America?"

The pastor shrugged. He clasped his hands under his chin and held his face, grim. He wanted to roll his eyes, but that would have been ungodly.

"For one"—Sani wagged his index finger—"which idiot here would marry her? You know Esther has been trying to marry her off." It came back up just then, all that he had swallowed, all of those years. Something was wrong with Amina—something hard to say. She had been a scattered child, restless and unreachable, Sani thought. Try as he might to contain it, the venom that encased his feelings had begun to leak.

"Your own daughter, hehn. Okay." The pastor had seen every permutation of family dysfunction, from mothers sleeping with their sons-in-law to children trafficking their own parents. Even with all that, this stunned him—the extent to which Sani went to protect the illusion of reputation.

Word of Sani's theft and the lies he told to conceal it spread quickly, in every community—Esther's, Amina's, Oyin's, and his own. And just as swiftly, two camps formed: those who knew Sani was lying and were willing to say as much, and those who knew he was lying but were afraid of what saying so would mean for their own standing. In this latter group were Sani's wife and a few of his friends. For better or worse, they would remain with him. And soon enough, they went about tearing Amina down.

Sani's new wife, Mary, Amina's former classmate, was the fiercest critic of all. Once upon a time, on There but for the Grace, she had been Amina's good friend. They did what girl-friends did: follow each other home from school; do homework on each other's beds; compare stories about whose mum was in fact the craziest. But it was Amina who did all the sharing. Mary asked the questions, plotting for a time just like this. She had not had any special interest in Sani, but she knew a vain man when she encountered one. A teenager, she had already learned that little flattered a man more than making him believe he was a prize that hadn't been adequately earned.

"I mean, an important man like your father." Mary had pushed the pretend microphone under Amina's chin. "What made your mother finally say enough is enough?"

"Well, frankly, I think she was just tired of being treated like the house girl. The cooking, the cleaning." Amina pointed around the room. With Mary, it was like having a sister—but one with whom she was free to say the things she was not allowed otherwise. "Esther couldn't take the nonsense anymore sha, so divorce it was!"

"There you have it folks," Mary continued in her fake news-caster voice. "We have just confirmed live that Esther could no longer stand Sani's jagbajantis. Aaand cut!"

Now, Mary said Amina was just ungrateful. "No matter how much he did for her, that girl would complain about something. Amina was always like this, full of drama." For those who needed cover for sticking with Sani, believing Mary gave them that. "If I'd had a father like Sani, who provided everything, I would have been thankful," she'd said. "In fact, I thank god for him now. Why would he need to steal from Amina?" Mary couldn't be blamed. She was living a good life, and would never know the extent to which Sani sacrificed and fronted to provide it.

Soon, Sani's loss would outweigh any pleasure he might have derived from trying to control his daughter. Once he lied to Amina and held fast, she vowed never to speak to him again. The final time he called, she answered, silent. After that, she refused his attempts to reach her. And Sani kept trying—an odd effort, given he'd accused Amina of lying.

"What could he possibly need to say to me? Short of him telling the truth, I have nothing else to discuss," Amina confided in Esther. Her mother was relieved, no longer having to explain why distance from him was the best course.

Only to himself, Sani would admit he was surprised by Amina's resoluteness. If his trying to meet with her betrayed a crumbling psyche, her steadfastness in rebuffing him towered in contrast. And that was what haunted him most: that Amina now saw him as he might have actually been. Unworthy of her presence.

⌣

"SOMETIMES THE LIE IS worse than the original sin," Sani's Lagos pastor preached to the congregation. Sani sat in the front pew, one hand fidgeting with the collar of his agbada, the other tucked tightly into Mary's lap. The pastor had paused on *sin* and looked at Sani straight on. The church mumbled a cautious "Amen." Even among those who claimed to believe him, the stench of Sani's fallibility lingered.

He could have squirmed his way into an explanation for taking the money in the first place. He'd fallen on hard times and needed it—some variation of that truth. He had a temporary break with reality and didn't know what got a hold of him—Satan was a reliable go-to. He might have also said that he lied because he was embarrassed by his desperation. Had he done the latter, he would have discovered that Amina could accept this weakness because she had it in her too. But Sani's sense of himself—righteous in all his ways and blameless in everything—was greater than any potential reward of contriteness.

So, this was the state of things when Amina boarded the flight to America. She had stopped speaking to her father and was unsure of the extent to which she still considered him kin. Some months later, when the sordidness of what he did finally trickled some regret into his heart, Sani sought updates from Esther about Amina's well-being. He wanted to know, but couldn't ask, how Amina had managed to buy her plane ticket after all. He hated that he had to go through Esther for everything concerning his daughter. But he accepted that he'd demolished any other choice he had.

Esther saw the aftermath of the lie in Sani's rapidly graying beard. And she was glad. Months on, she paid a special visit to Sani's church in Lagos for the end-of-the-year worship—just to witness his decline up close.

At the conclusion of the service, in the back of the church, they finally came face-to-face.

"Esther," he said, with a nod. His wife, Mary, turned her head the other way to show she wasn't bothered at all.

And though she already knew the answer, Esther asked anyway. "How have you been?"

"I can't complain," Sani said. "God has been merciful."

Esther, of course, understood that merciful was the opposite of what god had been to Sani. *Sooner or later, life will give you what you've earned,* she thought. Sani was no different. She almost felt sorry for him.

"I'm glad to hear it. Happy new year to you and your wife."

It was a terrible year for Sani. No amount of anguish would move him to the truth. Yet his failure circled his thoughts. Scripture felt stale. The writing in his journal was no reprieve. Sani was caged. Even then, he couldn't—or wouldn't—admit that dismantling that one lie might have been the way out.

AMINA

Shells in the shape of teeth

WHEN IT FINALLY HAPPENED, I WAS LIKE THE PSALMIC dreamers when god restored their fortunes. I understood that it shouldn't have happened to someone like me; destiny appears to favor the already blessed, we are told. But if I believed in the fates, they might have decided: *Amina, it's your turn!* And having nothing else, I agreed. My dream had come true.

My cousin Fatima and her husband Rashid had moved to a city in the American South. The people there, it was said, looked much like us. They enjoyed okra and greens in their stews, and spoke in tones that held traces of our own. It wasn't as cold there as other places in America. "But the nights can really chill your bones," Fatima had said. She would give me some of her old clothes for the colder months. She told Esther that I shouldn't pack too much. My mother said it was because their house was small and Fatima must have been ashamed.

My mind ran years ahead to life in America: a job as soon as I arrived and a flat of my own. On the telly shows, everyone had things of their own. Why wouldn't it be the same for me? I would design clothes of the finest fabrics and sell them out of a flowery boutique. America would let me do anything.

I'd spent my life on the verge of leaving, even when I had nowhere to go. But here I was, finally. Everything I could take, I spread on my bedroom floor. Clothes, most of which I had sewn, were laid out in descending order of style. I would make my mark through the things I wore. Bright greens and blues, shiny reds with glossy whites—these were the colors in ankara print that lit the clay in my skin. I put the photographs beside the portmanteau, unsure which to take. I wanted my children to know who I was before I became their mother.

1. Me: wrapped in a white blanket in Esther's arms at the entrance of St. Ruth Maternity Hospital.

2. Me: kneeling at the bank of Harvest River, picking up a rock.

3. Sani and Esther: dressed in green aso oke, posed on their wedding day.

4. Oyin: in blue overalls, and me: in a pink dress, standing with Sani in front of his Peugeot 505.

5. Me: propped against a wall under a staircase for a first-birthday photo.

6. Esther and me: in the kitchen at the old flat on Elekuro Street.

7. Esther: in the driver's seat of her Beetle on the day she brought the car home.

8. A photo of a danfo, with goats, in the middle of a market.

I put my mother's ankara scarf at the bottom of my handbag.

"I just wish you became more," Esther once said.

Even now, her words begged: What more could I have been? I could read by the time I was three. I listened to her troubles long before I understood. I tried to make her proud. What more could I have become? If something in me still needed waking, America would do it, I hoped.

I pulled a box of books from under the bed. A young girl looks out over a village hill. Head wrapped loosely, she is painted in swirls of muted tones: Tambudzai in Tsitsi Dangarembga's *Nervous Conditions*. I longed, with Tambudzai, for a way out of home. I put her, *So Long a Letter*, and *Butterfly Burning* in a side pocket of the portmanteau.

"So, when were you going to tell me? Right before you board the plane?"

Oyin's voice emerged in the room, softly, as if there the whole time, awaiting its turn.

"Of course I would have told you sooner than that. I just didn't know how." It wasn't true. Oyin already had Sani and Esther; America was mine alone. And she wouldn't have found out until the end.

"Don't say that." Her voice became louder now, more aligned with fighting. "I knew you were going to say something just like that, but you know it's not true. You really think you can live this kind of fantasy life, Amina." She threw a hand at the side of the room, as if that was where my fantasies hid. "Ignore the things that affect everyone else, turn away from anything that makes you feel bad?"

"No, I don't think that."

"Okay, so what do you think? Tell me."

"What do you mean, Oyin? I don't know."

"*I don't know*," she mocked in return. "I think you do. Leaving your mother by herself. I mean, how can you be so selfish?"

"She wouldn't have wanted to go. It's not her dream, the way it's mine. That's exactly what she said. What else do you want me to do?"

"Oh, I see. She didn't want to go, is that right? And what happens when she becomes an old woman while you're gone? Will you rush back from your dream across the ocean and take care of her? Or is that for me to do?"

"Look, Oyin, I'm not you. I want a good life, beyond this place." I pointed to my bedroom window, out there, where I believed my dreams lay. "I want to become somebody. I won't live and die here, struggling the whole way through."

"You're not me? Listen to yourself, Amina! *I want a good life. I want to become somebody. I want this, I want that.* Who the hell do you think you are? Who doesn't want a good life? You think I want to work at Esther's Palace forever? Or are you just better than the rest of us who wake up every day and make the best of our circumstance?"

"I didn't say that."

"Of course not, why would you? You're too much of a chickenshit to ever say what you really think. Everyone knows that about you, Amina. You walk around with that lost look on your face like life owes you more than you're getting."

"And what does life owe you, Oyin? What does my mother or even my father owe you? At least Sani married my mother. What can you say for yours? Where would you be now if we hadn't taken you in? Where would you be?"

Oyin laughed a laugh that didn't match the rest of her face; though her mouth opened, her eyes didn't blink. "Well, let me burst your bubble, Amina." She stepped fully inside the doorway and unfolded her arms. "The visa lottery is just that—a lucky chance. Nothing you have done or been makes you more deserving of it than anyone else. You will eat, shit, and die just like the rest of us. But when your time comes, you will be all alone. And you will remember I told you so." She turned and left the room.

I know now I will never see Oyin again. Behind me, on the field of the dome, is a family of two sisters and their elderly mother. They had escaped together when the waters rose past the first-floor windows of their house. The three women continually ask after one another, taking turns to find food and water. I wonder if Esther, Oyin, and I would be as close now, had I made a different choice.

There is a feeling that has caused me a subtle, persisting shame: I have wanted to be with and within myself free, no desire for the presence of another soul—not even my mother. I have known, without anyone saying so, that this longing makes me disinherited—not truly African, not a real Nigerian, not a genuine Yoruba child. If righteous and acceptable wanting must be in relation to one's kin, then I have been wicked.

Had I been confronted before this moment, I would have denied this feeling was within me at all. But Oyin was right that I turned from the things that troubled me. I was sure my desires were others' also. They were just too afraid to say.

Our culture reminds us that life will not go well for a child at strife with her family. In the single-minded way I pursued America, perhaps I have always been cursed.

⁓

NIGERIAN MOTHERS AND DAUGHTERS oscillate between formality and smothering. No amount of love can supersede the respect a mother is due. Offense is ever ready to be taken—it is a part of the culture that keeps things in their rightful place. Still, nobody loves their child like an African mother. It is a love unto death, for better or worse.

"Oh Amina, I am so happy," my mother said, when I told her I'd won the visa. But because the rest of the body doesn't lie, even when the mouth does, I caught the distress in Esther's eyes. And I didn't want to know the reason.

"I will give you the ticket money back, I promise. I'll send something home, each time I get paid."

"I'm your mother, Amina." Esther held my face. "I'm only doing my duty."

She insisted against it, and I insisted even more. Esther was the one who taught me that nothing in life came for free. Owing her my future was the price of duty, from which I was breaking away.

The days that passed blurred into the ones ahead. I packed for myself and added the things Fatima had requested. "Iru, kaun, koin koin, and honey beans too, if there's room," she'd said. Of course there was room. Fatima and Rashid were taking me in. Accommodating them would be my new way of life.

I had not dreamed of Sani since I was a child, trying to peek into his folded arms. In dreams of my mother, I cried a sound tight in my throat. Last night, in this dome, I dreamed I lay on a table in the way I am lying now. Esther, Sani, and Oyin held their cutlery over me, ready to eat. I float in and out of sleep, moving through water and time—nowhere and everywhere I have ever been.

IYANIFA: LAILA

Shells in the shape of a homing bird

I CAN TELL YOU THAT WHAT LAILA FINDS WILL BE grander than her dreams. It's about time. The shells tell me so.

⌒

THE LENGTH OF THE FLIGHTS—from San Francisco to London to Lagos—made Laila tense. She wore her loosest pants; anything too tight around her legs, and they would swell.

"I'd encourage you to get up and walk the aisle once every hour," her doctor had said. But it embarrassed Laila to be the person other passengers had to get out of their seats to let by. She wore the prescribed compression socks and hoped for the best.

If nothing else, she was sure she'd brought enough things; not for herself, but for her mother's kin, who were expecting gifts. "Don't go empty-handed. Everybody wants something," she'd been told. Even if they didn't say so, the family would be disappointed that she had nothing for them to provoke others' envy. "People are struggling," they'd said. And anyone coming from abroad—America especially—had to give.

"I'm struggling too," Laila had responded.

And she was quickly set straight: "No. Not having cable TV or an iPhone is no struggle at all."

Laila pressed herself into the window of the seat that had been chosen for her. The man to her right sat perched, ready to chat. It was his first time, too, going to this new place. He wanted to share it with someone—anyone—the jolt of excitement, meeting his fiancée for the first time. At forty-eight, he had given up on marriage ever happening to him. So had his family. Then he had met twenty-three-year-old Iyabo, who—he'd admit—was out of his league. "Dude, you're punching!" one of his buddies had said—joking, he hoped. Iyabo said her father was a Nigerian prince. He was still undecided whether to believe that, with the usual scams and all. But here he was on a plane, about to find out for himself.

Laila dug inside her purse for nothing in particular, hoping the look of busyness would dampen his eagerness. At Heathrow Airport, she had expected it—Black people, presumably Nigerians, going to Nigeria. But the smattering of whiteness made her wonder about their business here. Did they also have family awaiting their return? In the rush of passengers and flight attendants, no one else seemed to be bothered by the foreign faces. Most were preoccupied within the reach of their hands—maneuvering overstuffed bags or children that needed to be corralled.

Laila was grateful that the old man would be waiting when she landed. She couldn't imagine being in another country all alone, especially this one. How would it be, stepping out of the airport and into the open city air? She wanted to feel what others said they had felt when their feet touched the African earth—walking with all who came before, embracing the history in her blood. She reached for the plastic bag of letters in her purse. Of everything she'd brought, this was what her mother's mother might want most.

⁓

YEARS AHEAD, LAILA IS RETURNING. Amina, though, is arriving into a calamity that was never hers to defeat—not in this life.

Part III

The Storm

IYANIFA: JOSEPH

Shells in the shape of dreams

JOSEPH CURSED HIS FACE IN THE CAB'S REARVIEW MIRROR.
A mix of old and new betrayed the convergence of time.
Grayed goatee and riverbeds of crow's feet; salt-and-peppered
hair. When he smiled big, dimples sank into his laughing lines.
A hint of boyhood lit Joseph's eyes. He had little else to show
for his twelve years in the city.

At 5:17 AM, it was still dark. But there Maryam was, behind
the counter, making a first batch of the dark roast. Joseph
would have to go inside the café. And no matter how their
talk went, whatever she might say, he would stop in for coffee
tomorrow, and every day after that. He had no reason to end it,
other than he'd lived long enough—forty-five years—to know
when things just weren't working. Maryam was a sweet girl.
At twenty-eight, of course she was, with no kids and Joseph
helping to pay her rent. What she might have hoped for with
him, he couldn't say. His not asking, even after eight months,
was deliberate. He didn't want the work of knowing, and then
having to do it. Joseph held the steering wheel and waited out
the dawn.

THE CONTOURS OF JOSEPH'S morning rarely changed. The routineness of it, the busyness it made in his brain, helped him forget all the things he hadn't yet achieved. Sleep offered sweetness that bittered as soon as he woke. He'd chosen the most grating alarm setting to counter his wishful dreaming.

Back pressed against the toilet lid: √
Sink water pooled in his palms: √
A tight smile to check brushed teeth: √
House slippers switched for driving shoes: √

Joseph did these things every single day.

TWO SUMMERS AGO, Joseph had discovered the West African club scene: a Tuesday and Saturday night of Afrobeat and reggae in a rented auditorium with a deejay that played rock and hip-hop on the other nights. Joseph was leaning against the wall, waiting for the bathroom, when he heard a girl ask another girl to pretend to know her so the "creepy old dude in the suede jacket" would leave her alone. He turned to look at the man that had been described, and he was about ten years younger than Joseph.

"Ugh, like you would even give him the time of day," the second girl said.

"Right? It's always the ones old enough to be your grandpa." On *grandpa* the first girl had held eyes with Joseph, and he instantly understood that he, too, was the prototype they hoped to avoid. Then the girls high-fived and laughed, heads thrown back. Comfortably—no longer strangers.

Joseph went back. Not to that club, but to the two others in the city. He left his leather jacket at home and assumed his actual role: a mostly attractive middle-aged man hoping to meet a woman who would spend time with him. Beyond time, he didn't know what more to want; the years had dulled the brightness of his longing.

Two or three of the women he'd met at the clubs were young enough to be the daughter he didn't have, and by the third coffee date—because that was all they would agree to—they were sure: *Joseph, this isn't going to work.* This was after their teasing about Nigerian scammers and observing that *Joseph is such an easy name to pronounce.*

And then he'd met Maryam—at the café where he bought coffee, on the way to his morning shift.

"Maryam," she'd said it plainly like that, and held out her hand.

He thought it might be a sign, biblically, since his name was Joseph. Nothing else was remarkable about their meeting, but when one decides something is meant to be, everything surrounding it must be exaggerated for emotional effect.

Being with Maryam had been easy. Their times were spent doing together the things they would have otherwise done alone. They brought each other along for walks and food in the tiny places the locals called "holes-in-the-wall." One restaurant, owned by a famous jazz musician, ignited Joseph's love for gumbo—the okra and shrimp reminiscent of his beloved ila stew back home. After a late-evening dinner, he'd carved MARYAM into a tree with his pocketknife.

Joseph liked that he didn't have to put too much into the dating thing with Maryam. And he liked that she didn't mind at all. As the months went on, Maryam gained the confidence of a woman expecting to take first place. She'd imagined the hovering and elbow-pushing of faceless women also vying. Except there were none. Joseph just had the ease of a man who was happy with what was, not needing more.

Never married, no children, living alone in America—for an African, a Nigerian, a Yoruba man his age, this was an affliction past shame. His condition was best tackled with prayer and scripture. Joseph's mother mailed to him, express from Nigeria to New Orleans, three plastic bottles of imitation spring water; with them, the handwritten instructions:

Joseph—

1. Hold the bottle firm in your right hand.

2. Begin to walk around your apartment,
   stepping with authority.

3. SPRINKLE THE WATER ON EVERYTHING!

4. **Read Psalm 35:** Shout it very loud, exactly 7 times.

5. The prayers will seep into every crack
   of your life, Hallelujah!

6. You must open all the windows
   when you do this, Joseph.

7. Satan and his minions will flee in
   the Mighty Name of Jesus.

8. Each curse against your potential
   marriage has been broken, AMEN.

9. It is well with you, my dear son.

JOSEPH LAUGHED, BECAUSE WHAT else could he do? He put the bottles in the fridge and tucked the piece of paper into the pocket of his workbag, just in case.

TWELVE YEARS SINCE HE'D arrived in the US, and still he hadn't obtained citizenship. He'd applied for the visa lottery back home, hoping in America he could go further with his master's degree in engineering. The UK had been his first choice, until he heard that Nigerians were doing even better in Louisiana. The ones already there helped the newly arrived with a place to stay and a minimum wage job that didn't require too much talking. Joseph loved that about his people: at home they were ruthless, but abroad, they'd look after one another, few questions asked.

"Americans! They like to pretend they're deaf when they hear your African accent," his cousin had said. "Even if your English is better than their own, they will act as if you're speaking in tongues. But don't mind them. My son, George, he's making a good life for himself there." George repaired cars for taxi companies while putting himself through school.

"Drive a taxi? Ah, that's easy. I've been driving since I was twelve." It wouldn't be as easy to tuck away his engineering degree, he'd later discover; but back then, Joseph was a beggar, unable to choose. His cousin promised to get in touch with George and see what could be arranged.

George, it turned out, was a talented and busy mechanic. He and another young man from home, Rashid, operated the garage. By their third year in business, half of the taxi companies in the city took their cars to George and Rashid's Auto. Once the main business was full, they started another on the side: renting out cars as unregistered cabs to anyone unable to meet the city's licensing requirements. Of course it was illegal, but George had the right contacts, and he paid enough for them to remain quiet. The way he said *I just want to see my people get ahead* stoked the persistent melancholy of the newly arrived. *I mean, as Africans*—he held the center of his chest—*I want us to prosper, you know?* And that is what happened: every driver—mostly Africans—that worked for George and Rashid's made a good living. Bills were paid, families were fed. And anyone who knew about the shenanigans looked the other way.

But for Joseph, in those early years, the threat of trouble—driving a taxi without the proper license—kept him shy of peace. He'd imagine a police car at the edge of the road; before his next breath, he'd hear his heart inside his ears. This wasn't back home, where a timely offer of a bribe could avert legal consequence. He'd slow down, giving one less reason to be stopped. A few blocks away, he'd settle again into the comfort of his body.

Years on, the taxi was not his. He made payments to George and Rashid, both to rent it as transport and to own it outright. But Joseph lived more lavishly than he could yet afford—costly meals, business-class flights with Maryam—and for that, he couldn't remain consistent with payments, however much he tried.

Of the jobs he could have taken, this one let him be free. Picking up and dropping off passengers, he could add another entry to his mental tally of "All the people I've met," which at last count were from thirty-two countries, forty US states. Driving alone, he saw the city as he wished to be: forever moving, in and out of the presence of others. Houses in their jewelry-toned grandness, black iron balconies like ornamental webs, and those ceiling-high windows!

This wasn't the America of his childhood dreams. It was better. He hadn't thought he would see people who looked just like him, and—in the way he heard them talking, in the tone of Yoruba—sounded so much like him. In his years here,

Joseph had come to love the city, and he was happy to drive, just to be a part of it.

⌒

ON THE MORNING he was actually pulled over, Joseph hadn't spotted the police car on the side of the road. The abruptness of the lights in his mirrors; the way the street slowed in motion; the loudness of sirens over everything. All the times Joseph rehearsed the stop in his thoughts, it hadn't been as frightening as this. If he said or did the wrong thing; if he said and did everything he was supposed to—he could meet his end just the same. He pulled off the road and gripped the top of the steering wheel. His fingers slid from sweat. He held on and pressed down; he prayed to the air.

The officer knocked on the window. Joseph was careful—with his left hand he rolled it down, slowly.

"License?"

Joseph asked if he could reach for it.

The officer said that he could.

He handed his license to her. Despite the armor of uniform and the confidence of stance, she didn't look older than twenty. But there was the gun in its holster, within fingers' reach.

"Kunta Kinte, abracadabra!" The officer dipped her head into laughter. "How many names you got?"

Joseph's face went hot. About this, too, he'd been warned: the making fun that Americans do—of African names, of words unfamiliar, of things they have to stretch their minds and tongues around to comprehend.

"All of 'em is a mouthful. You African?"

"Yes."

"Yeah"—she nodded—"I knew it! I know an African at my church, uh huh. From Kenya, I think. You from Kenya?"

"No."

"Your name sure is a mouthful though."

Joseph nodded.

"You know why I stopped you?"

Joseph shook his head.

"Some knucklehead drove off in a cab after fucking up someone's car. You heard anything about that?"

"No." He watched her face for a hint that she might request the credentials of his taxi. Then he'd have to rifle through the glove compartment.

She stared at him a long few seconds. "Well, all right then." She held out his license.

"Thank you, officer." He watched in his side mirror for her to get back inside her car, and wouldn't move until she did.

Joseph was one of his several names, though just three had made it onto his license. He'd had six, at birth. The funniness of them to a white person, he guessed, had been his saving grace.

⌒

TWO WEEKS EARLIER, before this morning when Joseph would end things with Maryam, Rashid had shouted over the opened hood of Joseph's taxi that Esther's daughter, Amina, was coming to America. That simple announcement buoyed Joseph's spirits, as if nothing in his life had ever been wrong. He'd felt so good, he thought he might cry. Though Amina's arrival had nothing at all to do with him, he wrapped his heart around it and set it apart—purposed it as something to anticipate.

More than twenty-five years since he'd seen Esther, Joseph knew little about Amina, except for the nebulous bits he'd heard between stretches of time. The shadow of his remembering, of Esther, had been with him. His aloneness lessened, thinking about that day with her—the watery spice of pepper soup, the candied scent of frying plantains, the way she'd touched his hand without looking. Amina would be something, flesh, Joseph could connect back to that time.

They might never cross paths. But should someone point out to her that he was Joseph, the one who had loved her mother once, he hoped she'd relay something back to Esther—even if it was just that he was here, living. From the day Rashid delivered the news, Joseph built what he wore, how he groomed, and where he moved on the possibility that Amina might spot him in the city.

⁓

THIS EARLY MORNING, after the toilet, his teeth, and the slippers, Joseph drove to the café in the waning dark. In the rearview mirror, he surrendered to his aging face. What else could he do? He was there for coffee, and—if the flow of conversation allowed—to end things with Maryam, finally. Parked outside, he rehearsed the breakup aloud. Not so loud that someone passing might think he was crazy, talking to himself. Just enough to ensure his tone was acceptable.

The coming of Amina had infused his days with unfamiliar excitement. There could be more to this life than dating Maryam and driving a taxi—what, he didn't yet know. Still, he'd felt it; and that feeling led him to this morning.

A man passed the front of Joseph's car and went into the café. Joseph would wait—a breakup wasn't something a stranger should overhear. He popped the glove compartment and flipped through his wallet. He turned back to the café. He couldn't believe it: Maryam leaned over the counter and pulled the back of the man's neck toward her. They kissed— and kept kissing. *One-two-three-four* seconds, Joseph counted.

Maryam came out from behind the counter and hugged him: *one-two-three-four-five-six*.

Joseph was hot, sitting there. And it wasn't the heater at his feet. It was in his bones, the rage that spurred how quickly he unlocked everything and jumped out of the taxi. As if stopping that man from kissing Maryam would prevent the aftermath: her telling him the next day, while he sat outside of her apartment door, that she wasn't in love with him—Joseph. That they needed to hurry up and finish the conversation because she was running late to meet her new boyfriend—Frank.

Joseph was already out of his car, arms tight at his sides and frantic about what he might do. He went back to the glove compartment. There, his serrated pocketknife. He walked up the curb to the man's car and began to stab. Sharp, deep punctures in each tire; quick, quick—he didn't have the time. He scraped the side of the car's bumper, peeling the paint like pencil shavings.

Joseph sat in the taxi, chest heaving, eyes burning. He turned the lights off and slowly pulled away from the curb. Minutes later, just as the sun rose, the officer stopped his cab.

<hr/>

HE WENT TO CONFRONT Maryam the next evening. She shook her head the instant she found him waiting on the steps of her duplex. "I told you not to come. My answer won't change."

"A text message? After all these months, you'd think I deserve more than that."

Whatever Joseph was looking for, Maryam said, it wasn't her. "I wish you well, I really do."

And because it was no longer possible, Joseph now wanted Maryam. He sulked in it—the depth of his wanting. Since yesterday, when he'd seen her kissing Frank, being with her had become important. More so than Esther, a memory of years buried. "Please, Maryam." He held her arms. "Think about it."

She looked at his hands. "Some lunatic slashed Frank's tires at the café yesterday morning. Don't tell me it was you?"

Joseph stepped back. "Of course it wasn't me."

She nodded. "You should be ashamed of yourself."

He felt something more than that. Regret: for what he did at the café, and almost getting caught; for losing Maryam as he would, just as he did Esther, all those years ago. Joseph hoped, still, that Amina would befriend him.

He left Maryam's apartment and went straight home—straight to the fridge and to the bottles of water his mother had mailed. He pulled the paper from his workbag and read the instructions again. He mouthed a prayer or scripture; he couldn't tell which, it had been so long. Perhaps there was more wrong with him than he'd thought. And if anything could save Joseph, this might be it.

AMINA

Shells in the shape of light

THE WAY I MET THIS CITY IS HOW I RETURN TO IT NOW,
in my remembering. That warm, heavy afternoon—voices
close, carried away, then fading—has lingered in all that would
come after. The back-seat window of Fatima and Rashid's car
framed each street like a scene. Cold from the inside air, I held
my sweater between my legs.

Even in America, things could be this way: bedsheets hung
over broken windows and metal doors as thick as jail-cell bars.
Then, just a block later, houses the size of a palace, forest-green
lawns and fountain odes to Greek goddesses. Just like home,
the rich lived their wealth wherever they pleased, the plight of
the rest be damned.

"This is America?" I asked Fatima, between the console.

"Ah, what?" Rashid yelled over his shoulder. "You mean to
tell me you don't see the dollars growing on those branches?"
He pointed toward the windshield, at the large, hovering trees.
On one was hung—deliberately, it seemed—a gigantic necklace of green, purple, and gold. I swore I'd been here before.
Rashid squeezed Fatima's thigh. "Maybe we should take her
back to the airport, abi?" He laughed gratingly, to himself.

Fatima smiled tightly through her nose. She reached up as if to stretch, and then shook Rashid's hand away.

"We'll stop and show you the French Market, Amina. Rashid is going to rent us a stall to sell small things, aren't you babes?"

Rashid nodded.

Fatima's English bobbed in and out of a Yoruba accent—slurred, as if grease stuck her tongue to the roof of her mouth. "Those people will buy anything they think is from Africa." She leaned back and turned her head toward me. "Maybe we can sell fabrics too, and a few clothes?"

My heart sank all the way into my belly. Though I was just moments arrived, Fatima and Rashid's new car, their crisp clothes made me think I had set my sights too low on what America could give. I could be more than I'd been back home, I thought. Then again, everything good had its small beginnings. I would take my time.

"Yes, of course. I can design and sew too," I said.

"I know! Aunty Esther told us."

It was strange hearing my mother's name in a place where she couldn't be so easily reached. My fight with Oyin simmering still, I wanted to forget them all.

Rashid turned to the rearview mirror and smiled at me. Unable to see his eyes through his dark glasses, I was unsure how to receive the gesture. I avoided his face the rest of the way.

⁓

THEIR APARTMENT, 2A, was in the top-left corner of a grass-green duplex with yellow windows. The house looked happy, like a fable from a childhood book. It was larger than anything I'd dreamed.

"Does someone else live with you?"

"Just you, now." Rashid turned to Fatima and they laughed.

I looked up to the balcony and saw myself there in the early mornings, neck pushed out, willing the sun to rest on my face.

A blue staircase curved up to the second floor. On the other side of the wall was apartment 2B, where the old white woman with the spiky bob lived. From the day I arrived until the morning of the hurricane, she didn't say a word to me—not then, not ever.

The inside of the apartment was less happy—a bland, muted tan that darkened the mood in sudden contrast to the exterior. Still, I couldn't believe the amount of space just for the two of them! Three full bedrooms, each with a ceiling fan that worked when it wanted, according to Rashid. A bathroom divided into two rooms—a tub with feet in the middle of the larger one, a short toilet with a foam seat in the smaller. "You have to flush two times and hold it, or it won't go down," Fatima explained.

The sitting room had the expected furnishings, but without the garishness of those back home. A large velvety couch with fernlike print lacked a plastic cover to protect it from use. Fatima and Rashid even sat on it, tea in hand, as if unafraid of spills.

Just days in, I sensed Rashid and Fatima's was a house I could make home. And yet, for all my years here, I never would. The feeling had begun. It had always been with me: the certainty that I would never be as happy as I hoped. Even this would not live up to my dreams.

⁓

IF SMELL CONJURES THE memory of a time, taste is my way back. In America—in this city—I ate pizza and drank coffee for the first time. Of all the flavors and decadence I've consumed since, those two I have not forgotten.

On my third night, Fatima came into my room. "What are you craving for dinner?" She sat on the rug by the door. Surely now that I was an Americana, the jollof rice and dodo of the previous two nights were unsatisfactory, she teased. What was the one American dish I'd dreamed of, back home?

It still felt new, that wanting could be fulfilled, craving could be satisfied. "Pizza!" I sat up in my bed, excited for what was to come. "It's the classic American food."

"I think that might be a hamburger, but whatever. If it is pizza you want, it is pizza we will have." A local place made the pies from scratch and baked them inside a brick oven. "But forget that," Fatima said. "We'll get something good from one of the big, popular chains."

I didn't know the difference then—that it might have been better to eat at the local restaurant, that the quality of "small and family-owned" typically surpassed the large and wider-known. I'd been so pleased, so fortunate to be in this country, eating what real Americans ate from Pizza Shack! It is not lost on me that in a city world-renowned for the richness of its cuisine, it was fast-food pizza I once chose. I can laugh now, looking back.

⌒

I HAD ARRIVED TO New Orleans in early spring. A week into July, chatter began about the coming season of storms:

"Bullshit. They say the same thing every year: *This will be the busiest hurricane season on record.* And it never is."

A cashier and customer at the corner store exchanged doubts about previous seasons' warnings.

"Yeah," the customer said. "And you know who makes money with all that boarding up we do?" He pointed toward the door. "You guessed it! The hardware stores."

It was just like back-home gossip, but with the hurricane as the object of speculation.

I recalled the rainy seasons of my childhood—the flooding and eventual displacement.

"A hurricane is even worse than that," Fatima said. "It moves so fast. Before you know it, houses are destroyed and your neighbors are dead."

⁓

THE FIRST TIME I heard the sound, it came through the walls like whispers. Then long, whiny breaths, as wind inside a tunnel. The old woman in 2B must've forgotten the thinness of the walls. If there were such beings as seraphim, and if indeed they sang, they might sound just like this, I thought: sweet and unyielding. But this sweetness became like a brawl when the knocking began and eclipsed it. Something banging against the wall: a sofa, a bed, a table—wooden and sturdy. An even rapidity that insisted.

I held my mouth. The old woman had to know she could be heard? She couldn't have cared. I thought of my mother, who would've said she should be ashamed. I, though, envied her freedom—an urge for release that surpassed what anyone might think.

I pressed my ears against the wall—first, to be sure I had indeed heard as I thought. Then to listen, take it in. I almost did it myself: flip the hem of my nightdress and make room for my own ring finger between my fleshy thighs.

But then the sounds stopped. A pair of feet came closer to where I kneeled.

"You finally heard her," Fatima said, like she knew this day would come.

"Can you believe it?" I rubbed the middle of my chest and felt the ache—it hadn't yet left.

"Yes, I can." Fatima giggled into her hands. "I mean, we hear her sometimes. Even when she has the radio blaring, we can hear. You know she used to have a boyfriend?"

I shook my head; of course I didn't know.

"Yeah, she did. He left a few months ago, so she's a solo act now, I guess."

I had only been in the presence of sex while having it. And still it felt unknown, as if I'd never had it at all. Perhaps because it had been so long—no one since Niyi. Talking about it was strange. What more could I say? I looked to Fatima for the words. In the flatness of her expression, the formality she kept no matter what, I glimpsed our future. She would become to me like Oyin—present but impenetrable to the closeness I sought.

⌒

I WALKED THE STREETS of my neighborhood, alone, for the way the men called after me.

"African queen, my Nubian sister!"

"Goddamn girl, is that all you?"

"You carrying all them rice and beans, huh?"

"Can I take you to dinner?"

"Hey, you married?"

I had perfected my own version of Oyin's pendular switch of the hips. I did just as I pleased. Esther's trained, sussing-out eyes—the way they'd restrained me—were thousands of miles displaced. And yet, since the back seat of Niyi's car, there was little more than emptiness in the places I longed to fill. I hadn't even had a proper boyfriend. Here I was beginning again, yet for the first time.

From the corner of North Galvez up to Oshun Coffee on Esplanade, the every-now-and-again "How you doin'?" was less a question and more an acknowledgment of one passing stranger seeing the other, who was also trying to make their way. At other times it was a nod, to which I turned, smiling. Things didn't always need saying. In this city, all skin folk felt like kinfolk.

Standing at the counter, I was unsure what to order, so the woman behind it, Maryam, said she would make me the best drink I'd ever had. She was dressed like someone who had always been free to do as she wanted. It was the first time I had seen a white person with dreadlocks. Maryam's, fuzzy like fraying ropes, hung long and massive on her tiny head. And because Bob Marley was the universal blueprint for dreadlocks as far as I knew, these on Maryam's head, admirable in their effort, looked like a poor imitation. But I liked her smile, sweetly punctuated on both sides, just like Sani's.

By the door, a white man in a baseball cap waved for me to come over, I thought. The same hand gesture we use back home to say "come here" is used in America to say hello. He smiled when I reached him, but the tilt of his head and his long squint told me I'd misunderstood. "Oh I'm sorry, I was just saying hi," he said. How bold and silly I must have looked, walking up to a stranger simply because he had waved.

Maryam called my name, and I walked back to the bar. She handed me a cup of coffee lathered in cream, cinnamon, and vanilla syrup. For months after, however much or little money I had, this was the latte I drank. Maryam sometimes gave it to me for free. "You deserve it," she'd say each and every time. *Deserve*, I've repeated to myself since, more as inquiry than affirmation.

One morning, I searched my purse and found I didn't have enough for a latte. Maryam had the day off, so I settled for plain black coffee. And that was when I learned that coffee alone was no disappointment; the joy of its truer taste, light cream and no sugar, was unlike anything else in this world. The first sip—ineffable yearning. And once I worked out how to make it cheaply at home, poured through paper into a plastic funnel; how to carry it to the market in the disposable cups I'd taken from Oshun Coffee, I felt rich, like one of the lucky ones.

I MADE MY ONLY friend in this city at the wash-and-fold laundromat, about ten blocks from Rashid and Fatima's house. They hadn't asked me to, but I assumed the task of washing all our clothes every week. It was the least I could do.

I wonder about Dorothy's whereabouts now. That day, she watched me climb out of the taxi, clumsily pulling the trash bags of dirty laundry from the back. A string of underwear, tangled up in the hooks of a frizzy lace brassiere, fell into the street. I snatched it quickly, praying she hadn't seen.

From the corners of my eyes, I saw Dorothy move between the washers and dryers, as if looking for something to bless. The trash bags wrinkled from heat as I stuffed in just-dried clothes. Uninvited, Dorothy came anyway and held the bags open, making room for my beginner's efforts.

"If you need a ride home, let me know. I got my truck in the back." And though my instinct was to say no, I thought I might let myself be helped.

Dorothy walked like the men, speed and confidence in her feet. She slung my bags over her back, threw them onto the truck's bed. I got in and sat all the way back, my elbow hanging loose on the open window edge. Just like that, I had forgotten to be afraid.

"You had a beignet yet?"

I had, once before, but I said no in any case.

We would go first to Café Jardin, she said. "I do this every Sunday morning, after laundry. Jeffrey, my husband, he doesn't like sweet things. I don't know how he survives, to tell you the truth." She turned to me, laughing. I smiled back, hoping it was what she sought.

"You can fill your cupboards for less than twenty dollars. Beans, rice, enough meat to get you through the week," Dorothy had said, on the way to Save-A-Bunch. "I bet you didn't know that, Ms. Amina." It was from her I would learn: to buy a lot of food for a little bit of cash. I never had to ask Rashid and Fatima for more than they paid me to run the stall.

Did Dorothy make it out of the city? I had waited too long—in the chaos of deciding where to go, where it might be safe to ride out the storm—to find out. She'd said Jeffrey worked for the state or something like that. I hope he would know where they should go.

⌒

I FOUND IT ON Bayou Road while wandering, looking for a place where I might buy something with scent, something warm like a candle: Our Collective Bookstore. These dragging hours in the dome, reflecting on my first months in the city, I can't remember now what drew me to push open the glass door and go inside.

I saw Aunt Rosie right as I walked in. She sat on the carpet, swamped by a gaggle of toddlers gathered together, doing solo acrobatics.

"Well, Amina from Nigeria, welcome," Aunt Rosie said, arms open at her side, after I introduced myself. "This is the only bookstore here for people like us, and owned by us too." She looked down her glasses. "Look around, see if there's something you like."

I browsed for a while, trying to decide. Aunt Rosie walked closely behind, eager to help. I would leave with a book about the foolish escapades of a young man trying to get a job in the city while living under the rule of his anxious mother.

"Lots of dunces like that here, especially in the government," Aunt Rosie had said. "I can say that 'cause I'm old and I don't give a shit." She laughed and handed me the book. "This'll give you some idea of what you're up against."

⌒

THE NEXT MORNING, Rashid forgot to take his lunch when he left for the auto shop.

I told Fatima I would take it to him.

She didn't want to trouble me, she said.

I insisted. Besides, I would get out of the house and see a new part of the city. Only to myself could I admit I was curious about George and Rashid's Auto.

I arrived to the charming sight of men at work. Studiously bent over car engines, gallantly convened in a corner telling loud stories—rags slung over oil-smeared shoulders. Rashid waved at me through the glass door that separated the garage from the office. An older man with a goatee—must've been the one they called Joseph—sat across from him at a desk overrun with receipts.

"I can take that." A young man, late twenties, reached for the bag of food I'd brought. "I'm George," he said, wiping his hand on the side of his singlet. "And I already know you're Amina."

"That's me!" I was embarrassed by how big I smiled. But that didn't stop me from making the sort of eye contact—soft and unflinching—that declared interest.

"Welcome to America, Amina," he said, just as formally as the agents I'd encountered while passing through immigration and customs at the airport.

Maybe it was the sex coming through the walls the night before; the strings of my red halter dress tickling the small of my back; the angle of sunlight and the hope it evoked. I wanted George.

"AMINA, DON'T EVEN THINK about it," Fatima had said, when I asked her to tell me more about this George. "I know he doesn't look like it, but he's just riffraff that wormed his way into Rashid's good graces."

I had already thought about it. It was too late.

George was distinctly plain. I had seen him just briefly at the garage, but he carried himself like he'd never had to convince the world of his worth. Fatima was sure to tell me he made everyone—not just me—feel as if his universe of interest revolved around them. The most important thing was that, in the way he talked to me, he gave me what I was after: the pleasure of feeling desired. In turn, I overlooked anything that needed ignoring.

When I saw him again a month later, the afternoon he came to drop papers off to Rashid, I decided I could have him. I caught every bit of charm he threw my way: head-cocked smiles, deep-voiced laughter. George was so easily attained.

"I'll show you around," was all he said. Trite, but back then it had felt divine. Even if it wasn't, I knew how to make it so. I was practiced at it, the art of tending too much to the least effort by a man, as one might to a baby.

In the grip of loneliness, which came most often at night when my head ached from delayed sleep, I had prayed to be sent someone to love me. Then George arrived.

THE AFTERNOON I SAW a jazz funeral for the first time, it reminded me of the egungun festival of my childhood.

"Egungun, egungun!" The *clang-clang* and *dum-dum* of metal percussion and drums grew louder and louder inside the house where Esther and I were visiting with family in Ibadan. The young man that had torn through the parlor, screaming, raced to the veranda. The rest of the men walked quickly behind him to take a look. The women and a group of children, of which I was a part, hung back, unsure what to do. Remain there or run into the bedrooms to hide? It was eewo, I had been told, for women and girls to look directly at egungun—the masked and covered embodiment of ancestral spirits, here on this day to warn, advise, and bless the earthly children. Egungun, dancing and jumping through the streets; egungun, draped in the finest ceremonial cloths, tight netting concealing his face; egungun, pieces of metal fastened to his dress to mirror the glimmer of heaven, to which the souls have ascended. I was forbidden to look—it would result in barrenness or death, they'd said—but I longed to peek. And so I did.

⁓

I WAS IN MY ROOM, eyes closed on the bed, when I heard the horns, the singing and shouting.

"Where's the music coming from?" I ran into the living room where Rashid sat, rummaging through a jar of keys. "Can I go look?"

"Of course you can."

I pushed open the floor-length windows and stepped onto the balcony. There they were below, on the open road: a marching band of instruments and the young men and women who held them, in crisp white shirts and black pants. A small crowd, dressed casually in bright colors and feathered hats, followed behind, dancing and clapping.

I leaned over the iron railing. "What are they doing down there?"

"Celebrating!" Fatima said, from behind me. "It's a funeral. That's how they do it here, like a party. It makes sense, right? It's more like rejoicing than weeping, because death is never really the end."

Two days have passed since we arrived in the dome. Each hour, it becomes easier to think too far ahead, imagining the worst.

IYANIFA: ORUNMILA, THE ORACLE

ORUNMILA, TIME IS RUNNING OUT.

Have they not heard?

They have not heard.

Was it not told?

Of course it was told.

We will not rest until the girl has returned home.

We hope it is not too late.

And what of her mother?

What of her, indeed?

Did she not say what the Oracle pronounced?

She was silent.

Did the Oracle not warn that the girl must not go?

Of course the Oracle warned it.

Why did the girl go?

Olodu knows.

Was her mother there, at the beginning of time?

Of course she was not.

Can she claim to know more than the Oracle?

It shall never be.

Our Spirit will not settle.

Not until the girl comes home.

The girl must return to us.

Or she will return to the water.

ESTHER

Shells in the shape of turbulence

AMINA.

A strange thing happened as soon as you left. The prophets, the babalawos, and the iyanifas joined in agreement: the older souls that birthed the younger ones are to blame. For what? I will get to that shortly. To understand the present, we must return to the beginning, our culture says. Let me take my time, so that by the end of this letter, nothing has been left unsaid.

Not since you were a child, when I was married to Sani, have the streambeds of Harvest River run dry. And now it has happened again. It is a reason for alarm.

What I am about to say, I should have said on that day you came. I should have said it even sooner when I first knew, a few years before: you were not to go to America. Iyanifa had said it plainly like that, a pronouncement from the Oracle, Orunmila.

"She is a child of this land," was the way she put it.

Yours, Amina, is a destiny tied to the people from which you came.

"Some are made of this soil and it is with the soil they must remain," Iyanifa told me.

"And what about the others? The ones who go abroad and don't come back. The ones who marry and have children with foreigners. Are their lives not bound to this land too?" I demanded to know.

"No two people have the same fortune. We are not the ones to decide," she had said, as if that was that and the matter had been won. But she was right. In our culture, some are marked for a thing that must be fulfilled. The earth that moves under our feet also moves in the children of the land; their bones are like dust. Heaven joins the earth and their bodies. When one is displaced, the other cannot rest; when they are parted, a disaster is coming.

Well, I did not want to believe Iyanifa then, and not even after you left. But when the things that are happening now began, when Harvest River ran dry and the animals fled, I accepted that she had heard as she said. I am afraid of what more may come because I didn't warn you sooner.

If I tell you that the Oracle says you must come back home, that my own spirit tells me it is what you must do, Amina, will you listen? It is impossible that I still hold the deity-like power that Nigerian mothers are said to have over their children. You will not return, and I blame myself. I have not instilled in you the same weight of loyalty that I had for my mother, and which she had for hers. Or, if we are honest, this is a yoke you have shaken and will never pick up again.

I think now of the way I tried, from birth, to mold you to believe in the power of a god you cannot see, but who rules everything nevertheless. God is like the air, Amina—whether you believe in it or not, it commands life all the same. I hope you will find comfort in the divine.

⌒

I BELIEVED YOU COULD make a life for yourself in America. You could have more than me; even more than Sani had, when he had been somebody. That is why I could not stop you from going. There is more.

You remember your childhood. The times Sani took you and Oyin in his Peugeot. Your days at the banks of Harvest River, running in the dirt with those unfortunate children. There is a photograph: Sani next to that car, you in your dress, and Oyin in the one pair of overalls she always wore. In the photo, Oyin smiles big and proud, and there you are with your neck hanging low like an old woman shouldering the world. You and Oyin are the same age, but you look so much smaller. Not just in stature, Amina, but like you already believe life will be unkind.

We could all see that Sani's affection for Oyin was remarkable. Later, his second wife, Lara, was jealous of the girl. After Temi died, you remember that Oyin lived with Sani for a short time. Then, just as quickly, Lara would have none of it. Pressed as she was by Temi's family, she wouldn't say what it was that Oyin had done. The girl would have to go, she'd said. And that was that.

Then Temi's mother came and begged me. So I agreed to take Oyin. Whatever else was true, Temi had been my friend, once upon a time. I believe it is what any mother would have done. Someday, even you. That was the second reason I wanted you to go to America: to become better than a girl who lived in the shadow of her more desired sister.

If you are wondering what Oyin has to do with Harvest River, it is this: there are some children who are meant to leave their home and there are those who must stay. When I went to Iyanifa about the prospect of your marriage, it was Oyin, not you, that the shells conjured. It was not the way I had hoped the meeting would go. But Iyanifa insisted on speaking the truth of what she saw.

"Amina is not to leave this country," she had said. When the opportunity came—and it certainly would—Oyin was the one who was to go to America. It was her destiny, in fact. "And you must help her," Iyanifa said. "If Amina goes, you must know that she would be stealing her sister's birthright."

I could not tell it to you, Amina. I couldn't accept that Oyin might have a life greater than yours. I had the money to help her, but most of that I gave to you, after Sani's theft.

But as life would have it, it was Oyin that wanted to remain behind. And it was for me she chose to stay; she came and told me so, a few days before you left for America. I have sometimes wondered, maybe it is because of this one sacrifice that life has gone so well for her. About four months ago, she quit her job at my restaurant and opened a salon. Her shop has become the talk of the town, Amina. It is where the big and important women want to have their weaves and nails installed. If only you could see your sister now. She is full of sweetness—the meaning of her name drips from her skin.

⁓

HOW CAN IT BE that Harvest River has dried up again? The last two rainy seasons were the wettest, since Iyanifa became the regional barometer and began making her predictions. "But it is not water that the land is missing. It is the children. The children are gone and the water has followed."

"The children?" This was the question we all asked.

Yes, the children, she insisted. The ones who, when they were young, had made Harvest River their home away from their mothers' breasts. "And the water that has emptied from this land must have a place to go."

And how did she know it?

As with everything else, it was the pronouncement of the Oracle. Now we must wait to see if what has been said will prove true. I have heard of the seasonal storms in your city. I am afraid.

Amina, we are a line of women that dream. Before you told me of your plans for America, I dreamed of them. Before I was pregnant with you, my mother saw my belly in a vision. Last night, you were in my sleep. I saw a child's face and felt happy until I awoke. Maybe you will return, after all.

One last thing: stories travel quickly, even across waters. So you must know I have heard about you and George. Of course, I made my inquiries into his family. His parents are good. They are not quite illiterates, but their level of education is nothing worthy of a boast. George has no wife, no children, not even former girlfriends jostling for a ticket abroad. You might think this is good news, Amina, but for me it is a reason to reconsider matters. A man George's age without a life that can be traced? I am only saying go slow, and let us see what comes of it.

AMINA

Shells in the shape of forgetting

OUR STREET WAS A MIXTURE OF HOMES IN VARYING states of unfitness. The failing of Rashid and Fatima's house was the peeling paint that hung from the roof trimming like scabs. And like a few others in the neighborhood, their house didn't have the clout of a picket fence. Which trash ended up on our lawn depended on the day, who happened to walk by, and what they had in hand. Every other week, the night before the sweeper came to clean, Rashid tossed scraps of whatever had been left right into the road.

"You can't put that shit in the garbage can?" The young college boy who lived across the street, the one who wore white-framed glasses and a child-size backpack, said this to Rashid, elbows leaning over his gate, just feet away. "Come on, man!" There was a light smile in his eyes, the kind that made you unsure of the seriousness of what he'd just said.

This same boy had thrown a tangerine peel into our yard only the day before. Rashid, having seen him from the window just then, raced outside and yelled for him to *pick that rubbish up right now! What are you, a goat?* The boy had giggled, pulled his cap down tighter on his head, crossed the street, and skip-walked into his house.

This time, Rashid stopped, and in that very African way meant to make a person ashamed of existing, he frowned into the air and then spit on the ground, not once meeting the boy's eyes. The boy looked to the stoop where I sat, jaw in hand, watching them both. He mouthed big enough for me to see: *I feel sorry for you.* Rashid tipped his head my way and tossed the remaining scraps over his shoulder.

The rest of the night, I wondered what it was about my circumstance that had made the boy feel sorry. Too, another feeling made its way into me: if things didn't go well here, I had nowhere else to go. Four times a week, I worked at the stall in the French Market, learning from Fatima how to set up and take down merchandise, and which phrases could lure the most reluctant passersby into buying something. Fatima let me have a say-so in the designs of the ankara dresses we sold.

Back home, my life in America would have been a dream. But the day in, day out of working for my cousin had seared a kind of hunger into me. Having met George, imagining what might unfold between us, I suddenly wanted more than selling clothes in a stall. While it hadn't been a way out for anyone I could name, education as *the way out* was something I'd heard, growing up. Maybe with a degree, I could do more than just get by.

At dinner the next night, I tried to bring up university. "So, I've been thinking—"

Rashid cleared his throat and wouldn't stop until Fatima caught on and excused herself to send a text message that couldn't wait, she said. Then he held his chest and ran into the kitchen for water. I wanted to laugh and point out the absurdity of it all, but I held my tongue. It was as if they had sensed what was coming and were determined to shut it down.

After a few minutes, I cleared the table and took everything to the kitchen. Rashid was already in their bedroom. Fatima's whispering to him stung. I turned up the water and let the cups and plates bang, to drown out whatever they might have been saying.

Back in my room, I looked around at everything that was now mine. I thought again about the boy with the backpack. Perhaps he was enrolled at a college nearby. Within sadness for what might never come, I felt anticipatory joy for the desk I might one day sit at, doing schoolwork too.

⌒

I STOPPED CALLING my mother. This despite Rashid and Fatima reminding me that another relative back home had visited with Esther and insisted on knowing how I was faring.

"So, she still hasn't called her." Rashid, on the phone with someone, aimed his voice into the dining room where I sat, making notes in the margins of a school catalog. "I'll have a talk with Amina, don't worry." He hung up and came to the table.

"But I wrote back. Did she mention that?" I had mailed just two letters. The others, I couldn't yet send. One was filled with grievances my mother would deny: *I don't remember that happening, Amina.*

Rashid stretched his neck out to swallow. At the dining table, in the presence of food, he became interested in talking. "I'm not saying you didn't write, Amina." He waved his hand, which then expertly landed on the plate of buttered toast. He clawed two pieces. "But I didn't hear anything about it. You know it's about how things look anyway. So please, I beg you. Call your mother, Amina."

In our culture, a name is repeated both for emphasis and to invoke terror meant to bend the hearer toward acquiescence. Experience with my mother's attempts to frighten me—*Amina,*

Amina, Amina—had made me less afraid. I was steeled against Rashid's efforts.

Each letter I received from Esther ignored the substance of my previous one. It was as if we were starting over, every single time. *Amina, you should know that I have heard some things,* she'd written once. *You see, I don't want to go into them now. When you finally call me, we can discuss.* But the promise of gossip hadn't been enough to persuade me, and so in the next letter it was: *Blood doesn't always make family, you know. In any case, I hope Fatima and Rashid are treating you well.*

I understood that Rashid's plea to call my mother was a defense of his and Fatima's intentions. "You know how your mother can be," Fatima had said.

I did. My life in America hadn't yet become what I'd hoped. Not calling Esther was a refusal to concede. I didn't have a name for what was wrong—the feeling of something like malaise. I prayed and waited as I had been taught to do. And still, nothing that was worth the cost of a call. Esther might tell Oyin about my disappointments; my sister would then say she'd been right all along. What prosperity could I claim, unable still to repay my mother for the plane ticket? I dug further into myself: *Why can't you just be happy?*

Perhaps it was the flatness of the days. Each one, in its sum, was better than anything I could have had back home. Yet none rose to the mountain of dreams I'd built inside my head. I had left my old life, but here I was, still unsure where I belonged. I stopped writing Esther soon after.

⌣

"YOU'RE A SMART GIRL, we know you are. But we can't pay you enough to afford it. I'm sorry."

Hearing for certain from Rashid that attending university couldn't happen, however much I wanted it, I could finally name the pain that would not subside: America was not the promised land after all.

"And if we don't have your help at the market, there's no way we can keep this place, with all the extra expenses after you came. Where would you live?" The warmth in his voice stayed just a hint, lest I think he might change his mind.

All of this—longing for more; loneliness, listening to the old white woman each night; feeling too aware of myself in the apartment with Rashid and Fatima—was my state on the afternoon George walked in, a month after we'd first met at the auto shop.

I heard my heart around me as he came up the stairs. He smiled, and there was that familiar gap in his upper front teeth, a staple in our culture—the mark of a desirable man. And how did I know, without knowing, that George could give me the world if I'd asked for it? Though I never would. His visit, lasting just minutes, stretched into the following days and consumed all my remembering.

I WAS MEANT TO meet George, I told myself. Never mind that things fell apart after three months of courting. But hindsight is not as clarifying as is often claimed. Given the choice, I would do it all again; even the steps that led me here, to the dome.

George was the first man to look at me—really look—since that long-ago prophecy. Likewise, he made himself seen. The prophet had said there was a promised land—I returned to this often. If George in America wasn't it, then there would be none at all. That I met him on a regular day, that nothing had announced his coming—that, that, that. *Signs*, I'd decided. And that "farmer" was the meaning of the name *George* held even greater hope. He was the one with whom I would grow my dreams.

I could make something of anything, of anyone. This, I had inherited from my mother. I hadn't ever needed a transformation that declared to the world that my life had changed. Instead, I took bits and pieces of a day—a word, a look, a dragonfly soaring in my path—and gave them meaning. I'd say a prayer and make a command for something good to come. That was how I lived. And when indeed something good arrived, it was evidence of the power I held.

I made George the place I had been striving to reach.

⌒

THE FIRST TIME we were in his bed, I felt out of my body, as one does in the midst of a dream coming true. There I was and there was George, with me. I had been found. I returned to god in times of joy, when I knew for sure he still loved me. My heart had reason for praise. I have not been as happy since.

George pulled me to his chest, and my elbows sank. He was a meaty man.

"I don't have to worry about your boyfriend coming in here with a shotgun, do I?"

I was flattered. Not only did he think I might be taken, he also imagined I was seasoned enough to have a boyfriend and still date him.

"Oh, George." I leaned my head to one side and rolled my eyes with too much drama to feign calm. "Nooo, of course not."

I needed a cleverer comeback. Did *he* have a girlfriend? But what man would bring up a boyfriend if there was a possibility he might get caught having his own lover? With these Nigerian men, one never knew. It was nothing extraordinary for them to have a woman in America and another or two back home. Still, I believed I was safe—Esther had confirmed as much in her letter about George.

"What about you?" I poked his arm and watched my finger vanish. "Will your wife wait in the bushes for me with a cutlass?" That was my best banter. Whatever George might have thought, I was no loose girl.

"Come now, Amina, don't be silly." But his eyes, they'd shifted. Between "come now" and "don't be silly," George's eyes had moved from mine to some empty space at the side of my face. In that bare moment, I knew I wasn't being silly.

⌒

THERE WERE TWO FRENCH MARKETS, separated and defined by the access the owner of a stall had to money and influence. The more structured, tidy section sat under a large wooden arch held up by curved metal beams. Despite Rashid's boasts about what he could do and who he knew, Fatima and I, and other women like us, tended to a stall that was the visual opposite of the prettier ones: a leaning square, part faded wood, part umbrella, that was dark during the day, even when the sun illuminated everything outside of it.

But we made the best of it, as we knew to do. Working there, I felt in some way a part of a village of women who shared homelands, along with the tiny stalls of great aspirations in the Market. Sometimes I strolled through the other units, browsing and trying to decide whether to buy. There was nothing like it: walking into the eye-path of flattery-tongued African women, my body tingling at the familiar sounds of English intoned like words we speak only when we're alone, with each other.

The women watched the back of me—white women, almost always—when I walked inside our shop to look for a thing they'd insisted upon. My ankara headscarf, wrapped and twisted too tightly into a knot, chafed the hairs at the nape of my neck. It embarrassed me that I couldn't move my arms without knocking something down—trying too hard to showcase the objects for sale, as if I were the very thing being sold.

"Ooh, that's pretty," they would say. Or "I love that one," when I guided them to bangles like what they'd described. "But do you have something in silver? I'm not really a gold person. Sterling silver?" they'd mime, as if the metal could be described through gesture. Invariably, they wanted what we had in some other form—another color, another metal, another pattern, another size. Our things, as they were, were never enough. And we African girls trying to please, moving as quickly as we could to land on what they might want, were the most exciting part of the bargain—the ultimate reason to purchase, in the end!

"I like things the way I like them." Fatima looked around the darkening stall. Breaking down, folding, and packing up: these sounds tore through voices sore from calling out *miss, sir, my sister, beautiful lady.*

In the way of our culture, I should have received Fatima's words in silence. And then I would have done all I could to ensure everything in our home and at the stall were just as she liked. It was the reverence she and Rashid deserved for giving me a home, a whole new life, and possibilities in America. Instead, the next morning, I arranged and rearranged until a little bit of everything we sold could be seen.

Fatima's resistance was the force against which I worked that morning, frantic as if pulling the buying women's power into my body. I set up early and stacked the printed cloths, the dresses, and the up-and-down sets into the neatest piles. No more than a few earrings hung from the tips of metal hooks. The white women could stand at the door now and see everything we had, just as it was. I was tired, killing myself to find that one item they hadn't really wanted in the first place.

⁓

THE SHORTNESS OF BREATH came on quickly. I thought I was dying. Fatima pulled me to the metal chair stationed by the shop door. Just as quickly as I'd begun gasping for air, I felt fine again.

"It's probably heartburn," Fatima said. "Here, drink some water. I'll go get tea."

I took a sip of the chamomile and burped. The sourness came up in my throat. Fatima had been right; I had eaten too many pizza slices the night before.

After a day at the market, after I showered, Fatima knocked on my bedroom door.

"Amina dear, are you all right?"

"Of course. Why wouldn't I be?"

"You're not yourself lately."

"I'm a little tired, but I'm fine. Really."

"Let me know if you need anything, okay?"

I nodded.

My menses was five days late. It was all I could think about. As soon as Fatima closed the door behind her, I ran to the toilet again, sure it had arrived. The discharge in my panties was sticky and clear. No blood.

Idling in bed the next morning, my mind went to the last time I was with George; to him telling me not to worry because he would pull out; to how he'd pressed the weight of his face into my neck and breathed—a breath so thrilling, I'd let my arms relax.

WHEN I BECAME PREGNANT, my girlhood came to its celebrated end—*mother*, in our culture, being the achievement that establishes a woman's worth. Memories of home sliced through the dark of night. A kaleidoscope of the past lit into days I hadn't yet lived. It was then I remembered that I had been here before. In this city, in this place. In the back of Niyi's car, in those days, these were the things I had dreamed. And in the nights when I flew, it was the French Market I flew to, tip-tapping the cobblestone roads, my life in America awaiting my return.

Every woman is different in the way she discovers what her body has begun, it is said. For me, it was the burning. Deep in the center of my breasts, as if someone had sparked a match there. Two pink lines—one dark and firm, the other wavy but true—confirmed what I already knew. I pushed the pregnancy test to the bottom of the can, below the cotton swabs and mucus-thinned tissues.

I told Fatima a week later.

"My god, Amina, what were you thinking?"

"A child's not the worst thing that can happen, is it?" My tears blurred the room around me.

"No, it's not," Fatima shook her head. "But with George?"

I didn't know George well enough to defend his name.

A few seconds later, Fatima's shock gave way. She sat with me on the bed. "Things happen, I suppose." She put her arms around my shoulders and pulled me in. "Even with the best protection."

I did not respond.

"You did use something, right?"

The shame would not let me answer.

MY BODY FELT LIGHT and outside of itself. But this wasn't the happy floating of hopeful expectation. Within days, I'd become kin to a fellowship whose *I-sacrificed-everything-for-my-child*, they believed, absolved them of the harm they had caused those same children. After the euphoric newborn newness and the endearing roly-poly of toddlerhood, a simmering frustration sets in, some women say. Because then begins the truest test of mothering: how to survive all those hours of a child's incessant needing. The way a woman, wanting to be vibrant and full of her own purpose, is worn ragged as early as waking. Feed, comfort, serve, worry, and devise: this will be the course of her days. Until.

What would it mean to bear and raise a child in a perpetually skewed world? A girl, no less. I would want for her what mothers want for daughters: to do better than me, but not so well that I, who gave her life, might be cast aside. Sacrifice must have every opportunity to lord itself over the freedom of a forgetful child.

And years later, the urge to steer her course would have crept in. I would measure our lives, one against the other. Then I would have to answer, finally: Could I allow my daughter to become someone I could never be?

⌒

AS IF THE NEWS had been delivered telepathically, with a warning of the weight it contained, George disappeared. Just as magically as he'd walked in that lovely afternoon, he was gone. Even a whole world apart, I couldn't do better than Esther after all.

At first his phone rang and rang. By the next morning, it was a quarter ring and then: "George here. Leave a message." I listened to his voice at least a dozen times. I hung up and called again and again, willing him to pick up just this once. I felt alone, as in childhood when my parents left me to go fight in their bedroom.

Remembering it all now, nowhere to be but inside my thoughts of how these years unfolded, Fatima acted strangely from the moment I became determined to find George.

"Amina, we were all fooled," she'd said.

"Fooled by what, exactly?"

"Thinking he wasn't married. I mean, how could we have known?" She clapped her hands to the air, as if she was the one accused. "All these years, not once did I hear anything about a wife back home. Not even a girlfriend."

"George is married?" Suspecting it was one thing; having it confirmed was brutal. "So, did he go back to Nigeria?"

"You're asking me, Amina?" She shrugged with a hunching of shoulders so high, the intended effect fell flat. I didn't believe her. "I'm telling you, I don't know. He's not answering the door at his apartment. Rashid hasn't heard from him since last week."

"What then, is he dead?"

"Of course he's not dead, don't be crass!"

Rashid came home. For all the years they had worked together at the garage, for as close as they had been, for the brothers they had all become, he didn't know where George could be. I envied the convenient and sudden ignorance of men.

"I went to look for him myself. I was there fifteen, maybe twenty minutes, banging on the door. To be honest, I don't think he was there. I don't know. Maybe he went back home or he's just confused. You know, with everything." He looked at my belly.

"But he must have told you something, when you heard from him last week?" I couldn't believe that George's marriage was news to everyone else, as it had been to me.

Rashid scratched the side of his neck. "We talked about business, a car that needed extra work. I don't know what else to say. He should have told you he was married."

"How did you find out?"

"The usual, gossip back home—an old friend of mine went to school with his wife." He looked again at my belly.

I felt hopeless, in spite of his pity or because of it.

"I'm sorry, Amina."

Alone was no longer a feeling. It had become my life, fully.

⁓

BIRTH WAS HARD for all the reasons that are told; mothering has been nearly impossible for all the reasons that aren't.

The bleeding, after birth, was like dying. I nearly fainted from the red in the toilet the first time I went to pee—crimson mixed with yellow, stretched and bubbly, hung from my vagina into the bowl, like okra mucilage. "Don't worry," the nurse had said. "The bleeding is normal and it's not as much as you think." Instead, I panicked and called the labor and delivery unit after each and every trip to the bathroom. For five days, I wore a pad the size of an adult diaper to hold the deluge. Still, during sleep, blood trailed from my crotch all the way to the bottom of my spine. Fatima, tired of changing the sheets, I imagine, cut two big trash bags and spread them under the towels beneath me.

As if by hormonal magic, the morning I was discharged from the hospital, my breasts had grown to twice their size, hard and heavy with milk. "You're engorged," the nurse had said. "Feed your baby whenever she wants it, and when she's sleeping you can hand-express into the bottle like I showed you." I was surprised by how easily the baby nursed, and how good at it I seemed. Despite my fear that tiny breasts like mine couldn't make milk, they made more than enough. Very quickly, my baby grew big and round.

⁓

WHEN I GAVE BIRTH, I finally remembered my mother. Isn't this what daughters eventually do?

With Rashid and Fatima hovering at both sides of my hospital bed, I called Esther. We were six hours apart and separated by a mix of weighty feelings. Me, proud of the outcome: birth, the promise of new beginnings. Her with plenty of room for blame, still. If the hope of mothers is that their children will have an easier life than them, Esther's had been dashed. I have never thought that my father loved my mother; but at least he was there, distant as he was.

Rashid and Fatima were also there. They asked to be the baby's godparents. Had this been another time, or back home, it wouldn't have happened that way. At first, they would have been kind, praising god for his goodness.

We give thanks, O. Ah! A new baby is a blessing, they might have said. Just a few weeks later, they might tally how many hours I would have been able to work had I not been at home with a newborn.

If I responded that a new baby needed its mother, then: *Hmm. Okay, we understand*, they might say. *But you see, the bills don't know how to pay themselves*. And Fatima, who needed rest from recurring dizzy spells, wouldn't be able to run the stall all those hours, especially in the heat. *But god will make a way, don't worry*. Then they might stoop to the obscenely petty, leaving receipts on the counter for the amount of food I'd consumed since I'd been home from the hospital.

Instead of all that, they were kind. They had wanted a child of their own, and it just didn't happen, they said. This must be god's way of blessing them, having the chance to help raise mine. It would be their honor. Fatima patted my arm. And although I didn't ask, they understood that I would need the help.

What could I say but "thank you." Even when Fatima held my baby too close to her breasts. Even when I came home one time and she burrowed into Fatima's shoulder the moment I reached for her.

⌒

THE FIRST YEAR OF Laila's life was the hardest. My imaginings of having a baby hadn't ever moved beyond snuggling a warm, gurgling, heaven-scented creature. I didn't remember women's talks about the delirious, sleepless nights. The shocking helplessness of not being able to soothe a crying newborn—the frustrating dead end of *what to do, what to do*. The persistence of being alien within your own wholly changed body. The surprise diaper rashes despite globs of A&D cream. The sudden and inexplicable fevers, despite no other symptoms. Then fearing they might just die, in the midst of sleep, for no reason at all.

One horrible night, breast still hanging out of the neck of my slackened shirt, I felt for Laila beside me, where I'd left her just minutes before. She was gone. I vaulted over the pillows on the edge of the bed and ran into the hallway, screaming, "Where is Laila, oh my god!"

Fatima jumped into the hallway, her hair bonnet sliding into her face. "Amina, calm down, what happened? Where's Laila?"

"I don't know! That's what I'm asking you. I can't find her."

"What do you mean you don't know—where did you put her?" Fatima pushed me aside and went into my room. "Lord have mercy, Amina, she's right here in her crib! Have you lost your mind?"

I might have, because I didn't remember anything that happened after I'd laid Laila beside me to nurse. When had I put her back inside the crib?

"Seriously," Fatima said with a pitying headshake, "I think you need to get some sleep."

"Oh, you think so?"

Despite the common admonition to never wake a sleeping baby, I picked Laila up from the crib and held the warmth of her. I breathed into that sweet, familiar scent.

Everyone—cashiers at the grocery store, the unsolicited stranger waiting at the bus stop—had advice about raising a baby. How to feed, when to sleep, which toys to buy, what to do when they're sick. If one person was sure a particular approach was the best, another insisted the opposite was true. A voice in my head commented unceasingly about the right- or wrongness of everything I did. Never quite sure of anything, I just tried to survive.

I was tired from deep inside my bones to the edge of my skin. A near-fainting kind of fatigue that sometimes felt like the end of life, though all I needed was sleep. My first week home from the hospital, Fatima would wake up during the night to bring Laila to me when she cried, still hungry after eating. Then, just like that, I was on my own. One day inseparable from the next—all the days bled into each other, all of time, a mass of lingering fog.

Sooner or later, with the balm of experience, I sorted things out. The internet helped, of course. As it turned out, everything about raising a child had already been written, somewhere. But the hardest part is much less a grievance, and more the impossibility of loving painlessly: a year in, I didn't want to live my life without Laila. And just twenty-seven, I would have to make something of both our lives. I didn't know how to do it—alone.

PERHAPS NOW I COULD begin to forgive my own mother for the things she had or hadn't done. She could have loved me into an easier life—helped me to be a child absent of the spirit of restlessness, maybe. From her, I had wanted a feeling of safety: first, that I was lovable in spite of my inability to make myself so; second, that things would be okay, even when they couldn't be. If my father and I had been joined by impermanence, then my mother and I were bound by fear.

Months into motherhood, I had come to think Esther must have done her best. I wanted to call and tell her *Mummy, I understand.* Being Laila's mother meant I could now see the ambitions Esther had denied herself in order to be mine. What might she have wanted, after leaving Sani? A child meant thinking beyond herself, each day.

Attending college, all the while working to earn my keep and caring for a suckling infant, was impossible—at least in the constrained universe I had made for myself. I took Laila to the French Market sometimes. Customers barely stopped by our stall on those days. Perhaps they couldn't take the guilt of saying no in the presence of a child also in need.

Though I couldn't complain—food and shelter were no small things—and their presence meant that I didn't fall off the slippery edge, Fatima and Rashid as godparents did not ease my worries about giving my daughter a good life. I hadn't spoken to Esther in months; I wanted her to pull me back in. *You can return home, Amina,* she might say. *And bring Laila with you.* But that is not their job, Nigerian mothers. They tell you to make the best of your circumstance. Work hard and pray to god for help. Go to church, give praise and an offering. But it might be spiritual warfare causing all your problems, you see;

in that case, you must fight back. And if your efforts fail, then *thy will be done.*

The morning after Laila's first birthday, I opened the dresser drawer, placed some folded pants one on top of the other, carefully and tightly, as Esther once taught me. My body was fully visible in the mirror. I had perfected the good-and-busy-mother uniform I'd seen at the playground: a fitted T-shirt under a denim button-up, jeans the right amount of loose, braids pulled back for ease. Beyond appearances, I didn't know how to make what was impossible for me a reality for my child. Working at the market stall week in, week out with Fatima, I could not lift us out of this needing.

This is America? I had asked Fatima and Rashid way back when, my first minutes in this city. *America is different for everyone*, I would say now to that newly arrived girl. *You can dream the dreams; the invisible hands of circumstance will allow or deny their coming true. And your lot has been shaping up since before you were born, in the absence of your knowing.*

I have a memory of Laila that has come to me again as we lie in the dome, still waiting. A week before the storm, we are on the balcony, Laila in my lap, my back against those huge windows. She holds my face and squishes my cheeks toward my lips. I bulge my eyes and she unravels into a giggle at me turning into a "Mama fish!"—which she screams, between gasps of laughter. I tell my mind to stay there; it is already working to not think ahead or back to something from the day before. But I can't help it: I wonder if, years from then, Laila will remember being happy with her mother.

"The big one is coming" was how they reported it, over and over, in the days leading up to the hurricane—the newscasters, weathermen and women, and politicians who made their on-air rounds, warning us to "have a plan of escape now!"

We were going about our days just last week. Then the volume of the news of doom, which had until then been low and in the background, suddenly began blasting on high. On the bus, at the French Market, chatting with the cashier at the corner store: everywhere, the hour had come. Fortune, too, changes easily like that. I knew then that the life I still imagined would never catch up to the swiftness of the disaster ahead.

IYANIFA: JOSEPH AND AMINA

Shells in the shape of the past

JOSEPH TRIED TO MAKE IT HAPPEN—BEFRIENDING Amina. He thought of it often and wrote about it in his journal, which he kept in the glove compartment, somewhere beneath the serrated pocketknife. He listened to the gossip between the men as they worked on the cabs. Even when he wasn't driving and had no official business at George and Rashid's Auto, he ended up there, coffee in hand, laughing every now and again at their stupid jokes and chiming in when the topic interested him. He prayed that someone would mention Amina soon, before his desperation pushed him to do so in some embarrassing way.

Finally, Rashid said he was having a dinner party—a kind of welcoming Amina to America. This was Joseph's chance to meet the girl face-to-face. When Amina had visited the shop some time back, he'd been in the office with Rashid and caught just a glimpse. This time, he would smile and be relaxed around her, he promised himself. And then he would find a way to subtly launch into talking about Esther without anyone thinking that was his sole purpose for attending the party in the first place.

Several days passed and none of the men said anything else about the party. At first, Joseph was calm. He quietly decided that it just wasn't meant to be. But after more days of nothing, he had the thought that the party was still happening and their silence was meant to exclude him. He became unsettled.

While the men laughed at another ridiculous joke, Joseph also chuckled. And then, in the middle of a wholly unrelated topic: "Sooo, what are we bringing to the dinner party?" he asked, too loudly.

The men looked at each other, foreheads crunched. Joseph didn't know what else to say. That one question, difficult enough to render casually, was all he had rehearsed the last few hours. He had nothing else.

"The party! Okay, I see." Rashid nodded. "We decided not to have it. Well, Fatima did. It was her idea in the first place. So, you know." He shrugged to punctuate the words and indicate that was that. The men went back to their loud jesting.

Joseph, unable to push down the disappointment, felt it as a tightening in his throat. He mumbled some reason to get up—not that the men noticed—and went to the bathroom in the back. The toilet was surprisingly clean for a place run by men, he thought. What else could Joseph do now but just let it go?

But the men weren't as ignorant as he thought. Each one of them—George, Rashid, and the others who sometimes worked there—knew of Joseph's brief past with Esther. It had been discussed more than he realized: how all these years later, neither he nor Esther had found love. Esther had at least tried with Sani, even if that ended badly. But Joseph's path, not having produced even one child, had simply been tragic, they thought. And maybe he had made too much of that one meeting with Esther in her mother's restaurant—in truth, he'd hardly known her at all.

Or god just forgot about Joseph. This is what most everyone thought about the matter, though not one of them would say it to his face. He was a good man; they agreed that his heart was worth the effort of their silence.

⌣

IT WAS A SLOW MORNING driving the taxi, circling the side streets for a hail, watching pedestrians, purposeful and striving. Something must have changed in Joseph within the last couple of years, because these things no longer filled his need for closeness with the world. He wanted a smile meant for him and a chance at mindless small talk. *Don't worry, she has today off,* he reassured himself about Maryam as he drove to Oshun Coffee.

His pep talk notwithstanding, as he opened the door he prayed that Maryam would be inside. She might be sorry now about how messily things had ended between them. And because he still had feelings for her and, well, everyone makes mistakes, Joseph would absolutely take her back if she even hinted at it. Never mind that Rashid had begged him to *please leave those white ones alone, and find yourself a good Black woman.*

Forget that nonsense, Joseph thought.

Maryam having the day off indeed, he found a table outside in a spot where he could watch everyone come and go. Being sought out, being found and asked for nothing—Joseph had never had that. He bowed his head over the free city newspaper and relaxed into the feeling of coffee and not-a-care-in-theworld. And then he heard his name in a soft, high voice.

"Mr. Joseph?" The young woman was already smiling at him when he looked up. That was what he noticed first: her bright smile and big earrings.

"Amina? Hello! Wow, it's really you. Have a seat." His words slurred together. Joseph pushed out the wooden chair across the table from him.

"Thank you, but I don't have much time. I just wanted to say hi. You came by the house last week, but I was in the kitchen. I've heard so much about you."

Joseph couldn't resist the "All good, I hope?"

"Yes," she laughed. "Of course, all good." Amina had not heard as much as she implied, but what else could she say, trying to be nice?

"I've heard about you too. Mostly from Rashid," Joseph said. He didn't know whether it was his place to say so, but "I'm really sorry about you and George," he added.

"Things happen." Amina waved her hand, to be cool at the mention of George. "It's been so long, thankfully." Laila was almost two years old, and Amina thought about George every day.

"For what it's worth, Amina, I didn't know he was married. I'm sorry."

"I'm surprised I haven't seen you here before," she said, ignoring his expression of regret.

Joseph saw Amina's reticence. She held the back of the chair, as if wanting to sit. She didn't seem to have anywhere else to be. But he didn't want to push.

"Is this your first time here?"

Joseph wasn't sure how to answer without getting into the embarrassing story of him and Maryam. "No," he said flatly. "I come from time to time. You?"

At least twice a week, she said. Sometimes more, since Oshun Coffee was just walking distance from her house. Then she asked how driving was going, if he liked the city. Yes, she liked it too, she said. But she was still getting used to being new and a foreigner at that. The food kind of reminded her of back home, though. But she hadn't made many friends. Not yet.

"How's Esther?" Joseph uttered the words too quickly for his brain to remind him that he wasn't supposed to mention her at all.

"We talked a little while ago, and she seemed fine." Amina had spoken to her mother only twice since the call at Laila's birth—part busyness, mostly embarrassment about George. Every now and then, Esther left a voicemail. Amina saved them all.

"It's been much longer for me." Joseph laughed, at a joke only he understood. "The last time I saw your mother, we were teenagers."

"What was she like?" Amina asked, genuine and curious. She knew little about Esther as a young woman.

"She was beautiful and serious, in equal measure." Joseph laughed again, betraying his nervousness. "I used to see her walking home after school, when Sani and I ran errands for work."

"You knew my father?"

"I did. We were friends." Of course Joseph couldn't tell Amina how Sani had taken Esther from him. It took years to forgive himself for not being the first to make a move; that was his failing. "But we lost touch over time." Truthfully, he couldn't handle seeing up close the life Esther and Sani had made.

Her parents had existed before her, she knew that, but it still surprised Amina to hear it. There must have been some drama, too, given Joseph's obvious discomfort discussing Sani. Amina liked Joseph—he didn't appear to be hiding something dark, as with the other men she had known.

"That's too bad," she replied blandly, about Sani and Joseph's friendship. Then she said she really had to get going. "I'm happy we finally met."

He was relieved to hear she had to go because had he more time, he might have said too much about wanting to see Esther again. Joseph held his hand out and shook Amina's. It was a little formal, but he didn't know her well enough to offer a hug or even a pat on the back.

Watching Amina walk away, Joseph felt fulfilled. He had finally met Esther's daughter! When he had least expected it, too, as is often said about good things happening. Amina didn't look as much like Esther as he'd wondered, but she was every bit as graceful. In her bright headscarf and glowing skin, she made him proud to be African too.

With all of that, Joseph had actually forgotten Maryam. Again. He no longer cared whether she had been at the café; it wasn't for her that he'd come, after all. God knew where Amina would be, and there, too, Joseph was.

⌣

GEORGE'S FATHER, WHO HAD recommended Louisiana to Joseph, was not his blood cousin. They were cousins in the way all Nigerians from the same village are cousins: they know each other's family name, and when away from home, they act as kin. When Joseph first met George, he was joyous to have a connection to his roots. George was eager to help Joseph make money.

"I told you, I know some people. Don't worry about it," he had said, when Joseph repeated his fears about driving a taxi without the proper papers.

"Listen, brother," Joseph had said, "I trust you know what you're doing. But understand, I can't afford to get deported."

"Deported?" George had sucked his teeth. "You're talking nonsense, man. Ask around. Not one person that's worked for me and Rashid has had any trouble."

And because George—at twenty-something—was young enough to be Joseph's son, Joseph treated him as such. On the occasional Saturday morning he took off from driving, he and

George met at the elementary school near the auto shop to play soccer. Joseph, having lost some of his skills with age and lack of practice, still liked to give George tips about his game. George—missing his own father, Joseph suspected—allowed him to assume the role.

The morning Joseph was pulled over on suspicion of slashing Frank's tires, he had called George first. "It's all right, man. Nothing came of it, and you're good, right?" George had said. And he hadn't chastised Joseph for being careless, flying into a jealous rage over a white woman.

It did not take long, though, for Joseph to notice that George was unnaturally private. Joseph was not a nosy man. But despite his sharing about dating frustrations and the breakup with Maryam, he knew very little about George's love life. It was through Rashid and the other men at the garage that Joseph heard George and Amina were dating. He had been so excited about what could come of it: George, Joseph, Amina, and Esther might someday be a family.

"Congrats, my boy!" he'd greeted George, as if his being with Amina had been a career achievement.

"Ah, it's nothing," George had responded with a sheepish head bow and wave of the hand.

Unable to get more out of him than that, Joseph did not force matters. Subsequently, he rarely asked about Amina and assumed no news was good news.

There is no other word but *shock* to describe what Joseph felt when he found out that George had vanished and Amina was pregnant. His hopes for a family—slightly delusional, he could admit—had crashed. He went to George's apartment and knocked until his knuckles swelled. For the first time, he allowed himself to feel the anger—Joseph almost cried. He sat on the doorstep and waited, still hopeful. After about three hours, well past midnight, he accepted that George was gone, just as Rashid had said.

⌒

THE DAY AFTER SEEING Amina at Oshun Coffee, Joseph felt happy. If nothing else, he thought, he could be like a grandfather for Laila. With that, he stopped at the French Market. He browsed the stalls until he came to a table of handmade dolls. He was pleased to find a dark-skinned baby with thick, curly hair just like Laila's.

"That's the one," Joseph said, pointing to the doll he wanted wrapped up.

"Here, I'll add a brush," the vendor said, putting a toothbrush-sized thing into the bag.

Joseph was excited! He weaved through the throng of tourists until he reached Fatima and Amina's stall. They were not there. Rather than wait for his shift to end, he drove to their house straightaway.

"Ah, Joseph, you just missed them. They walked to the grocery," Fatima said, pointing in the direction of the balcony.

Joseph's face tightened.

"Why don't you come in and wait?" She opened the door wider. "Join us for dinner."

"I hope Laila loves it," Joseph said. He would leave the gift bag rather than go inside. He wanted to make a few more trips before dark, he said.

Back in the taxi, the news on the radio barely touched his glee, thinking of Amina and Laila opening his present: a tropical storm rapidly gathering strength in the Gulf of Mexico was now headed for New Orleans.

This could be "the big one" everyone feared, the reporter said, droning on as if reading a script.

Joseph shook his head, doubtful. Last September, a similar prediction had been made about another tropical storm—he couldn't remember its name now—and in the end, nothing happened. All that preparing, all for nothing.

"I'm not worried," Joseph said to the open cab window, steady in his belief that everything would be all right.

⌒

ON THE MORNING OF the hurricane, Joseph had not decided what he would do or where he would go. He had lived in his apartment for five years, and for the first time, his landlord boarded up the windows. This worried Joseph. He'd heard about shuttles at several spots in the city, taking residents to the Louisiana Superdome. That would be his last choice. Joseph loved people, but not enough to be stuck with strangers for hours.

He filled one backpack with a few clothes, energy bars, and an unopened letter from his mother. Then he added a plastic bag with toiletries, and some cash that wouldn't fit inside his wallet. And finally, a few condoms. He wasn't sure what he thought might happen during this storm that the news anchors and even the mayor were calling "the big one," but he didn't care. He would be prepared for every possibility.

He flipped open his phone and dialed the shop's number in case one of the men was still there, doing last-minute work. The phone rang, then went silent. Joseph didn't really have friends, did he? He'd had the thought to drive out of town, but no one had invited him to go with them. And no one at the shop had asked of his plans or offered to ride out the storm together, as the locals liked to say.

George was gone, the sorry bastard. Joseph and Rashid weren't as close now, George having been the glue between them. *At least Amina will be with Rashid and Fatima,* he thought. He opened the contacts tab in his phone, to be sure those he loved were within his finger's reach. Joseph did not want to be alone.

IYANIFA: THE STORM

THE STORM IS HERE. IT CAME IN THE NIGHT.

⌣

AMINA HAS HEARD OF it everywhere, the last few days. She thought again about the rainstorms of her youth, and the warning that this, surely, would be worse. She and Laila would leave with Rashid and Fatima if it came to that. Laila would be safe so long as Amina was. And Amina would be fine because of Rashid and Fatima.

"Because they know the fragility of being far from home. They won't let anything happen to you," Esther had said before Amina left for America. Amina's faith rests not in herself, not in the city, not even in god—but in this new family, with whom she has made a life.

On the morning of the hurricane, a frightful hush blankets the city. Those who had the means to leave have done so. The ones who remain must now choose: weather it at home or in a shelter with strangers. In the market stall, Amina and Laila wait for Fatima and Rashid. Amina's trust in the unknown looms larger than what is true.

⌣

THE RAINS HAVE COME.

They pour heavy and make the ground like mush. Houses are whipped to and fro. Cars float above the deluge. Thousands of miles away from the city of green, purple, and gold, Harvest River holds its breath; its waters will return when this storm has ceased.

The authority in my hands notwithstanding, I cannot convey the breadth of the storm's coming wreckage—it is impossible. The shells tell me so.

⁓

THE RAINS HAVE SUBSIDED.

The city is underwater.

The dome is swimming with souls.

The days come and go.

⁓

THE STRAY DOGS GREW RUTHLESS, after the rains. When the power died, they walked and sniffed at random. Now, they charge and growl—hungry for what is left. On this fourth day in the dome, many are waiting to die in the grayish-blue dark. It is not hard for the dogs to get to the dying, weaving between babies crying for milk and arms cradling the shoulders of tired mothers. The stink and bleeding lead them there.

There is no more food or water. For hours, the dogs have picked at the remains of a fleeing soul. Their gums leak flesh, feces, and spit. They aimlessly circle the field until the rounds become smaller and smaller. Finally, they collapse in a corner on the prickly green faux grass, across from the main entrance of the dome.

When the doors are open, daylight streams in and you cannot see the dogs. But if you listen, you will hear the low and desperate snarl in their throats. Their eyes droop, heavy with something like shame. They, too, have become sick. The dome is damp; the smell, sour. The sweating air has left their hairs wet and stringy, as if drenched by a hose.

One has in his teeth, clutched between his skinny legs, a blue-and-yellow ankara head tie. A scarf, the kind that would adorn the head of a Yoruba woman; a short while ago, it did.

ORUNMILA, YOU WARNED of it.
The embankments did not hold.
The children's living places are submerged.
Even the animals have scattered.
>*Did they not know this disaster would come?*
Of course they knew it; it was predicted by their own oracles.
>*Why did they not prepare?*
This will be asked again and again.
>*We cannot lose our children this way.*
Nevermore.
>*We remember the ones they stole.*
We have not forgotten.
>*What will they do now?*
You already know: they do not have a plan.
>*How much longer before the children have relief?*
They, too, are asking.
>*Will the girl come out of it alive?*
Olodu knows.
>*And what about the girl's daughter?*
Laila will have a long way to go.

THE WIND-DRAWN RAINS POUNDED for hours. Through the tear they made in the roof, a thin stream of dawn projects a theatrical spotlight onto the faces of people lying in cots, wrapped in old shirts and newer blankets. Amina, in and out of an edgy sleep, traces the shadows of bodies in a paced, blurry stare. She reads again the illuminated words on the front of an old man's tank top: *There but for the Grace of God, Go I.* Laila's plaits brush under her mother's chin, her body gathered inside Amina's wringing fear.

They lie in the dome with the rest. The ones who could not make their way out—too ill, too old, no car. And the others who would not. Those with the choice: unwilling to trust whatever awaited them outside the only city they had known.

Amina vacillates. A warm draft swirls. The first inhale reminds her of the smell of hot, rotten food that lingers after the garbage truck jolts through the French Market streets on Tuesday mornings. At the back of her throat, she tastes sour urine and the stench of sweat. Word comes and drifts away with the bringers of the word, who arrive and depart as quickly as the messages they bear: *Help is on the way. Food is coming soon.* Neither is true.

A mother's second self is born when her child enters the world. The death of a daughter is an end and a beginning again. The shells tell me so.

AMINA

Shells in the shape of an end

MAMA.

Mummy.

Esther.

Laila and I have been waiting in the dome for more than three days.

I have remembered my growing up, how I arrived to this city, and the last three years. I am telling it all to you; the end urges me back to the beginning. The past is sharp and returns in its right order. But you will want to know how I came to the dome and what has happened here. The last few days, the hours in between, are a bit disjointed—but I will try to recall, as practice for when I see you again.

It is hot, and the sounds are hard to bear. Something seizes my thoughts: a smell that springs up, the pitched cry of someone who is dying or afraid of it. If the things I tell are scattered, it is because I'm drifting, forgetful of what I have already said.

Laila is here in my arms; she remains the center of everything. She is small but wise. Her eyes miss nothing at all. All of this will be with her in the years to come. She will tell it to you, whatever I have missed. When you meet her, you will feel as if you have loved her before. And maybe you have. She has your confidence. Even Sani's charm—even Sani. I haven't spoken to him since he took the money. It is an ugly way to lose a father.

⌒

IN THE DAYS BEFORE the storm, no one was afraid. For those who had been through it before, the warnings to leave weren't different from what they had heard in the past. At least that is what they said. Some would ride it out with family in other parts of the state, or farther west, in Texas. A hurricane by itself isn't a thing of fear—not around here, where people have learned to go on, whatever the world tosses their way.

The year before, we had driven to Mississippi to avoid a hurricane that turned out to be a tropical storm. Another time, at home, we weathered a storm that was more severe than anything I had ever seen. But beyond a daylong power outage and some downed trees on our street, we came through it fine.

On August 29, the morning of the hurricane, the air was grim. Confidence turned into double-checking windows, documents, backup plans, and who to call if nothing worked out as hoped. Even those who said they'd been there, done that, had to assess things anew. The rest just had nowhere else to go.

Rashid and Fatima had asked me to run the stall early that morning, hoping to catch the last tourist surge before things quieted. There were always a few who remained in the city, refusing to go home, certain they were braver than the born-and-raised. I would pack up by late morning, and Fatima would meet me with the van so we could load our merchandise and leave the state. That was the plan. But as soon as I arrived, I noticed the emptiness in the market; the people who were usually there were already gone. The flow of lingering tourists was just as slow. All of it was strange.

The Edge of Water | 175

Laila was with me. Fatima, who sometimes watched her on the days I went to the market, said I should take her this time. She and Rashid needed to get plywood to board up the garage. Laila toddled on the pavement, the absence of shoppers enabling the freedom her wobbly legs desired.

The storm would pass through the city late in the night, the forecasters had said. I clicked on my phone: no missed calls. The market was deserted. Around 11:00 AM, I called Fatima. No answer. I tried Rashid. The ring went to voicemail.

Laila and I are waiting for you, I wrote. *Everything's packed up.* Five minutes later: *Are you still coming here or should we meet you somewhere else?* My stomach turned. Where would Laila and I go? I thought about Dorothy.

And right then, a woman I had seen around the market walked to where I stood, holding the diaper bag and Laila's hand. "There's a shuttle two blocks over, taking folks to the dome." She was headed there, she said, and Laila and I should come too.

"I'm waiting for Fatima," I said, hopeful still.

If we missed this shuttle, there would be another in an hour, she said. She turned to leave. "Don't worry. By this time tomorrow, it'll be over."

I hoped so. I had packed just two days' worth of clothes and diapers.

I called Dorothy, and the phone rang and rang. I dialed Fatima again. The line clicked, dead. *We're headed to the dome,* I wrote, for the last time.

I heard this once, and I am afraid now to know if it is true: at the moment of death, it is said, the last person we call upon is mother—in the name we have given her. Mama. Mummy. Esther, I cannot see the day after this one, or the one after that. My mind has gone black.

IYANIFA: JOSEPH

Shells in the shape of solitude

UNABLE TO REACH ANYONE HE WOULD HAVE WANTED TO be with during the storm, Joseph got in his taxi and drove. Zigzagging thoughts, two U-turns, a last-minute jerk of the wheel to the left instead of the right—all of this led him home, where he parked his car and then walked down the street to take a shuttle to the dome.

Now stuck, exits blocked by army guards and police, Joseph had little choice but to believe this was where he ought to be. He looked around the field. He stared at the faces that looked back, as if that might reveal an answer to the questions in the air:

"How bad is it?"

"When are we gonna get out of this hellhole?"

"Is it safe to go back?"

"I just wanna go home."

Like the tens of thousands of others, Joseph was a drop in the sea of sweaty white T-shirts and dark brown faces. Off the field, he found an empty seat. He tried to relax into the waiting, but his legs wouldn't stop their tapping. He turned his wrist again to look at his watch—he'd already forgotten the time from just a minute ago.

Several hours passed while Joseph slept. Amid the sounds, loud and grating, what woke him was the soft heaving of a child, trying to catch her breath. He picked up his phone: no missed calls. He asked around for the latest and some man pointed to the roof, where sharp light streamed in and rain fell through. He scanned the space. Only faces and faces.

He would look for a bathroom, to give himself somewhere to go, a goal to meet. By the time he reached the hallway, he was sure the toilets he had imagined were no longer as they had been. Like the people, the smell had nowhere else to go. Joseph sucked spit between his teeth, but his breath wouldn't hold. The floor was wet—with what, he could not tell. Trash blocked his way to the urinals, so he headed for a stall. It was like that dream where he went from toilet to toilet, looking for a place to release, but each one was increasingly unusable—feces on the seat, debris floating inside the bowl, a bloody or slippery door.

He picked up a large plastic cup and sat it right side up. "Forget it," he said, and he did what—given the state of things in there—everyone else before him must have done: urinated right on the bathroom floor. When he reached the doorway, he wiped his feet on the jamb and went back into the hall, his chest out and back tight. He rubbed the corners of his eyes and tucked his shirt in. Some things would be lost in the days ahead, but he still had his pride.

⁓

DAYS PASSED. HIS EYES burning from scant sleep, Joseph couldn't tell at first what he was seeing. By the time she sharpened into view, a moment that would, at any other time, be lit with joy was instead subdued. Joseph held his arms to himself, unsure what to do.

Amina sat at the edge of the field, legs crossed, with Laila held between them. The girl pulled at her mother's neck. The scarf on Amina's head reminded Joseph of girls back home, the ones he grew up with but was too scared to go near. It was hard to find now, the strength to smile. But he did anyway. This was Amina, after all. And, too: Laila, holding under her tiny arm the curly-haired doll that Joseph had bought. Maybe it really was the end, given the day's effectiveness in digging up this sadness in him.

Joseph angled his head to better see Amina and Laila from where he sat, sideways in his chair. The way his clothes stuck to him, smells from his body, despair all around—he couldn't go to Amina. God knows he wanted to. But not now. When they made it out, he swore he would let her know *I saw you and Laila at the dome. I was too embarrassed to say anything.* And he'd be sure to ask *How does Laila like the doll?* Today was not that day. Of the regrets he would have in the storm's aftermath, this one would haunt him the most.

Joseph's thoughts sank. He had put his mother's letter in a plastic bag because he hoped someone would find her, if it came to that. He wanted them, whoever they might be, to know who he was—that his roots reached across the waters, all the way back to her. He hadn't wanted to think this way, but he was sure now that god had forgotten about him. If the water rose here, too, soon the people would drown. He closed his eyes.

⌒

JOSEPH MIGHT NOT HAVE KNOWN, had it not been for the little girl's disturbing wail. The sound found him somewhere on the field where he'd lain down. It reminded him of the way he cried when he woke up and couldn't remember where he was or name the loss he felt. The silence that followed her scream, too, was like that loud quietness that trailed him to waking once in a while—a forlornness whose weight lessened as he came to.

He went in the direction of the crying. In the center of the hallway, near the bathrooms, a small crowd gathered around a body he couldn't see. Joseph walked to a breach in the circle that had formed. Fresh, clean diapers—visually distinct from all else around them—held tight under the body's slender arms.

There Laila sat, on the floor, rubbing her eyes and panting for air. A young man picked her up and handed her to a woman in fatigues. Joseph knew, then, that it was Amina who lay there, still. He motioned to the blockade of men that he knew the unconscious woman. Just the same, they waved him back and said that a nurse had been called.

"She's my stepdaughter!" Joseph yelled to the group. Anguished, he'd blurted what he thought might get Amina help. She belonged to someone who loved her, he wanted them to know, someone who loved her mother.

The men moved aside to let Joseph through. He kneeled beside Amina and held her forehead. He whispered what he thought Esther might say. His hand moving on her skin, she was still alive. A young girl as driven as he had once been; who traveled overseas to see what she could become. And this—her body on a filthy sports arena floor—was the answer to her dreams.

He couldn't believe how long the nurse was taking to arrive. Amina's breathing slowed. *What the hell's the holdup?* Joseph wanted to scream. But to whom? The crowd had already thinned, their attention trailing to another tragedy just steps away. The men in uniform turned their backs to Joseph. For all his trying, he had never wielded power in a critical moment. Here he was again, losing someone that mattered to him.

The nurse finally came. She checked Amina's pulse. Joseph asked for an update, but the surrounding noise drowned out his panic—the nurse did not hear him. Amina's body was taken away—where, he did not know. He searched for Laila, and she, too, was gone. He ran to pick up the ankara scarf that had fallen from Amina's head. A snarling dog grabbed it; it was too late.

〜

THE NEXT MORNING, buses arrived to transport the survivors. Of the fourteen hundred souls who perished in the storm, six had died in the dome. The twenty-five thousand who had been there for five days, now displaced, would be taken to shelters out of state until it was safe to go back home. Most would never return to the city.

That very evening, news about Amina entered the airwaves in the form of an interview: a white woman who frequented the French Market. One who enjoyed being sweet-talked to buy this thing or that.

"Yes," she nodded. "Yeah, I knew her, the African girl. From Ghana, I think." She looked over to her left, off-screen. "Oh, she was from Nigeria? Okay, yeah, well, I was close." She waved her hand, annoyed at the detail. "Anyway, I went to her shop once or twice. She was always super friendly. It's a shame what happened to her. We lost a lot too. Our house flooded while we were out of town on vacation. It'll take months to replace *everything*," the woman said, wiping an errant tear.

〜

JOSEPH WAS FORTUNATE. Within a week, he was home—his apartment, untouched by the disaster. On a walk one morning, he stopped at a newspaper and beignet stand. The front pages were still about the storm. He flipped through a few, searching as he had since leaving the dome for an article about the deaths there. He noticed that although Black residents suffered the most during and after the storm, a disproportionate amount of the hurricane reporting was about white people in the city. He had just about given up when he found an article mentioning Amina, not by name, but as "the young African woman who died, aged 28."

The *Fleur-de-Lis* recounted: Amina held Laila and went to look for diapers, somewhere in the direction of the bathrooms. A woman who had seen her body described her thighs and legs. Limp, formed into the shape of the number 7, thrusting from under the stall, and visible from the entranceway as if daring passersby to ignore them—which they certainly did.

"The bruise on the left side of her neck. The way her legs bent. She looked so frail when they moved her to the middle of the hallway," one witness said. These and other tidbits led the self-assigned experts to conclude Amina had slid and fallen at some point while stooping over the toilet bowl.

They were mostly right, the shells tell me: Laila's diaper had soaked through, onto Amina's pants. She tried, but could not find the young boy selling diapers. Maybe in the bathroom, she could salvage unused paper towels or something else to clean Laila's bottom, she thought. But all of the napkin dispensers had been emptied, and of course the faucets were dry. When Amina walked into the bathroom stall, it was not to use the toilet, but to see if any clean rolls remained. There were none. She turned to leave. With Laila still in her arms, she slipped and hit her head against the metal door.

Unaware of the minutes that had passed while she lay unconscious, Amina thought she was fine and stood up. "Where is Laila?" She looked about her. Under the sinks, the little girl was crouched inside an open cupboard, as if hiding to be sought. "I found you!" Amina, drained of everything, still managed this act of playful surprise. She picked Laila up again and walked out of the bathroom, into the hall. And there, coming toward her, was the boy selling diapers. Seconds later, she collapsed. Joseph and the others tried, but could not help her.

Her hair piled in a clump in the middle of her head, flattening toward the temples, where the ankara scarf had been wrapped. The dog, the one with the skinny legs, found and clung to it just moments after they took Amina's body away. When he finally dropped the scarf in the field, hours later, Joseph was there to pick it up.

Amina, whose name means "safe, protected." Amina, the conjurer of dreams; Amina, who wanted more than fate would permit. Amina, in horror and squalor, was vulnerable in the end.

ESTHER

Shells in the shape of silence

AMINA.

This, too, I am writing down, as if you will someday read it. I do not know how else to empty my mind of the things that remain unsaid. You will not respond; of course, you will not. But I have to think that so long as I say these things, you will hear them somehow. After everything, can I expect god to be so merciful? I do not know.

And I do not know what to do with this feeling. They say it is anger. But in the past few days, I have let myself feel it all the more. And now I am convinced: it is rage, and none of them will survive it.

The minute I saw them standing at my gate, I knew already the news they brought. By the firmness of their shoulders and the softness in their jaws, I could tell that the terror was meant for me alone. Rashid and Fatima must have been found alive. How else could their mothers and fathers have breath, strength in their legs to come to my door?

For three days after the storm, those of us with family in your city watched the telly, to see for ourselves how bad it had been. The mind will doubt, until the eyes can confirm. It was worse than anything our thoughts alone conceived. The water spread and rose in every scene. It is not difficult to imagine what comes in the aftermath of flooding. When the water recedes, all life is gone.

Whether my eyes are open or shut, this is what I see: an old man, a child with his young mother, the roof of a house, someone waving a shirt, faces in despair. Not once did the camera return to tell us of their fate. What happened to those people as the water rose and rose? I am thinking of it now and my chest is heavy with crying.

Were you also waiting for help? I am afraid to know. At certain times of the day, I am unprepared for the deluge—sadness, then rage. And then I give up. I piece together again the things I have seen and read and heard: that it was dark; that the food was rotting; that so were the bodies, even the ones that were still alive; that you might have slept in your own waste; that Laila had no water left in her baby cup when she was found; that the smell overwhelmed, with refuse stuffed in every inch. No air, no plumbing, no relief, nowhere to go. And where, in our culture, does a mother go with feelings like these?

And Rashid and Fatima. They are still alive. Every day they breathe, as if you were never a part of them. You must have never been—I see that now. How could they go on, otherwise? I, too, should be dead, but god won't help me. So here I am.

Of course I think I could have kept you alive. While you went to the bathroom, I would have held Laila tight. Then you would not have slipped from the weight of trying to keep her safe. I owe you what you gave to your daughter. Helplessness is impossible for a mother with empty arms.

It is different each day. Today, it is killing me that I will never be there. I will not know the stench, the heat, or the hopelessness of your last days in that dome. I only want to be a part of it, so I can understand. When I am lonely, I want to breathe with you your last breath.

⌒

I REGRET THAT I let you go. There is no other word for regret—I have searched and I cannot find it. Here, I failed to give you the kind of life in which you would have wanted to remain.

Rashid and Fatima, again. Their story has changed once more. This time, they say the phones died and they could not reach you while you waited at the market. By the time they arrived, you had already left. But why did they leave you and Laila on your own in the first place? Their answer has yet to give me rest. It is themselves they are protecting of course, but some of it shields me too. If I knew the truth, I would wither from hatred. My scorn would scorch anything good that could come their way. But in the end, I am the one who is burning.

The officials say they cannot send you home; there is not enough of you left. Where, then, did you go? Even here, we know of the hatred America has for people like us. I wonder if they would have tried harder if you were white. They found pieces of your things and matched them to photos from Rashid and Fatima. You are "unaccounted for," they decided in the end. This new name, as if you are no longer my Amina. There was a gap of time between your going to the bathroom and when the last bodies were recovered, they wrote in their notes. With the air as hot and wet as it was, with some of the animals that had wandered in, you were not the only one with nothing left.

I have hoped that, somewhere, there might still be bones. And on the days regret releases its hold, I grab a new thought: *Maybe it can happen to me, that my daughter will return.* Thank god for the glimmer that remains.

AMINA

Shells in the shape of vision

ESTHER.

Did I really do all of that—strive against life, come overseas, accept single motherhood—for this? I wish I'd lived my childhood, and each day, more slowly.

I need a diaper for Laila. She has worn the same one since the middle of the night, I think. I have lost track of the time. My phone died, our first night in the dome.

There is a man in baggy army fatigues, assigned to bring supplies, fix things that break, and somehow keep order within this restless crowd. This man has paced the field, back-forth-up-and-down, since we arrived. I use him, the moment he passes by, to mark the hours as they come and go.

"When does he eat?"

"Does he ever rest?"

"There he goes, at it again."

"Back-forth-up-and-down."

When there is nothing else, we discuss this army man.

There is a young boy by the bathrooms, I'm told. Or maybe I have already seen him. I can't remember. He's managed to acquire several packs of diapers and is selling them, five dollars apiece. A woman, who I assume is his mother, an aunty maybe, lies in a cot guarding the stockpile while the boy collects cash and returns change to his customers. I hadn't thought my money would be of any use here. But I don't blame the boy. He intends to leave this place and is already making a way. I envy his hope.

⌣

YOU WILL HEAR ABOUT the horrors of the Superdome, but anything you're told pales next to the truth. Hovering in our midst is darkness that is beyond an outage or the ability of a generator to prevent. It is more than the clogged toilets and the shame of bodies suffocating with waste. It's a dizzying pull into the thick of gloom.

I have not seen the pacing army man at all today. I think that is why I lost track of time. A few minutes ago, we found out where he went: to the top of the dome. He waited there until he thought no one was around. Then he walked to a ramp connecting two of the buildings. He jumped, nearly three hundred feet down. "Like flying," he said, as he leapt.

There are two main waiting areas: the large field of faux grass, where the games are played, and the surrounding seats that stretch all the way to the top. After the rains stopped, many were ready to leave. Unsure what they might be returning to, they were willing to take the chance nonetheless. But the guards, some military and others self-assigned, blocked every way out.

"Believe me, I know it's bad, but you're better off in here," one said. Having lost touch with the world, we only had their word. Eventually that assurance wore out, as had our patience and hope preceding it.

I have looked for diapers in every corner of this place. The boy selling them must have moved on. Laila and I just left the bathroom. The garbage was at least ankle-deep. We made it into the hallway. I see the boy now. There is so much noise, Esther, I can't hear my thoughts. My head hurts and I don't know why. Laila is clutching her favorite doll, the new one from Joseph. We finally met; he is a nice man.

"Get the nurse!" someone yells. A man is kneeling beside me, crying. It is hard to breathe.

⌐

I HEAR YOU IN my half sleep; you are talking to me, and I am a little girl. *There is no longer a place for regret*, I want to say. You have come to be with me, even at the end. I can't believe it now, that I stopped calling. I don't have an answer that will satisfy your *why*. I can only say we are no longer apart—you, through me, to Laila.

Esther, I know what is coming. It feels sudden and unlike what destiny had promised. A new life, yes; but the duration of it was never assured, god himself might say. I wonder now if there were hints all along. I admit I have lived from thought to thought—inhabiting what could be, never wanting what was.

This is not the end. Of course it isn't. Aren't you the one who said we are a line of dreaming women? I have this vision: there is a large rock in the middle of where our old streets meet, in all the places we have lived. There is where I will be.

IYANIFA: IMOLE

THE SHELLS TELL ME SO.

When the guardian elders are told that Amina has left the world below, they rush to Imole, arms outspread, prepared to welcome her back. They wait, not knowing what her soul will choose: a first lifetime with new kin at Imole, or transition to Aarin, the middle place, where a few souls retire.

In the early moments of her ascent, Amina will rest. Olodu will meet her later on the way. Her restlessness having been quenched, she is now a weary one.

No matter what Amina chooses, another lifetime with the five of them will never be again. Olodu has declared it. Their hands will not be entwined. The storm has changed that.

Part IV

After the Storm

IYANIFA: JOSEPH

Shells in the shape of shame

SIXTEEN YEARS AFTER THE HURRICANE, JOSEPH remembered. He placed everything on a timeline of before and after. "You and I met," he might say to a friend, "two years after the storm, isn't that right?" It was the point around which Joseph's life was fixed. So much more living had occurred since then, but he had not moved on.

Finally, he was driving with a legitimate cab license. A few months after the storm, he had tried to give the old car back to Rashid, who told him, "Just keep it." Even when Joseph insisted, Rashid said that he had paid so much on it already, and "Anyway, we all need some help right now."

Then he heard that Fatima had left Rashid; no longer a stall to run, she had filed for divorce and taken Laila with her to California. The last time Joseph saw Rashid, he said to his old friend, "I heard about you and Fatima. Are you all right, man?"

"Come on, you know me. I'm doing fine," Rashid had said.

But his thinness said otherwise. Patting his back goodbye, Joseph had felt more bone than flesh. A year later, Rashid sold the auto shop and returned to Nigeria.

⌒

ONE MORNING, JOSEPH WENT back to Oshun Coffee. For the longest time, he had weaved in and out, going at the hours he could avoid Maryam—the shame of the slashed tires still there. The server put his sandwich and coffee down and took the number off the table. The café, twisted and torn by the hurricane, had been repaired and repainted. In place of the mix of people who used to stop in for coffee were now white college students and older white customers, their parents' age. The coffee and food cost much more too. "And it's not even as good," Joseph said to himself.

He picked up his phone and searched for Fatima. He had been thinking about Laila. The last time he talked to her, she was about ten years old. Fatima had put her on the phone, to be kind, but it was clear to Joseph that the little girl did not know who he was. He'd heard Fatima in the background say "Doll," trying to remind Laila. Laila had whispered something Joseph could not decipher. Then she giggled and passed the phone back to her aunty.

Last night, Joseph had dreamed something he couldn't remember; this morning, he felt like his life was fading. He pressed the phone symbol and waited.

A bright voice filled the other end.

"Fatima, long time."

IYANIFA: LAILA

Shells in the shape of loss

LAILA KNEW FROM THE TIME SHE WAS SMALL THAT SHE once had a mother. It had not been a secret between Fatima and her, as she'd always called Fatima *aunty*. But while her mother, Amina, was not hidden, for Laila she existed mostly in her wondering of how a *mom* might have been. At their house in California, there were some photos in the plastic-jacketed album under the living room tabletop: a few of Amina at the French Market stall, looking like a child; two of Laila at the hospital, wrapped in a purple blanket, tiny and pale with dense black hair; and the only picture she could find of herself as a toddler—Laila with Amina, a week before the hurricane.

"Your mum's things are in the closet, if you want to look through them," Fatima had said, more than once. When, at thirteen years old, Laila finally decided to search the closet, nothing had precipitated it other than knowing Fatima planned to be gone all that day. She would have the ease to look through everything in her own way, in her own time.

There was so much in that huge leather bag, a catchall of Amina's belongings. Knickknacks, a wooden box of costume jewelry, like-new Yoruba-style clothes, frayed scarves, and a pair of old leather boots. There were more photos here too—ones

Amina must have brought from Nigeria. Laila was most curious about the man and woman in traditional clothes, of whom her mother seemed to be a perfect visual blend. If there had been a distinct smell to Amina, the years of her belongings stuffed into a bag had made it plain and old.

Laila felt alone, even with Fatima perpetually hovering. From then on, whenever she was out of the house, Laila returned again to the leather bag in the closet. During one visit, she found the photo that made her feel the closest to Amina's world, before America—the opened back of a bus in a market, with two fascinating goats. And then there were the three envelopes, unaddressed except for *Esther* written on the front, in her mother's handwriting she supposed, because Fatima did not write like that. The seams were rippled, like they had been resealed. Laila picked up the envelopes and shuffled—*one-two-three-one-two*. She put them back inside the clear plastic bag that had held them. She wanted to read the letters, but, in the end, would not. She didn't want to discover anything that could blunt her imagination of who Amina had been.

⁓

ON THE AFTERNOON FATIMA moved her new boyfriend into their house, Laila began her plan to leave. Then fifteen years old, she sensed the imminence of freedom she hadn't yet touched. There was something else too: Fatima had started telling Laila she was imagining things when Laila tried to correct Fatima's forgetfulness. The incidents were small at the time, but looking back, they were the onset of Laila questioning what she thought she knew.

Fatima said she had left a bagel on the kitchen counter earlier that day. "Did you take it?" she asked.

When Laila reminded her that in fact Fatima had eaten the bagel for breakfast and discarded the paper bag it came in—because Laila saw all of this—Fatima yelled that Laila was a liar. "You need to stop eating things that don't belong to you. Or are you a thief?"

Fatima raged about matters of varying importance, around the house and out in the world. It jarred Laila, being unable to predict when Fatima would lambaste her for something she was sure she hadn't done. Fatima's boyfriend, Henry, who had mastered his own silence, stayed in the background and *out of the business of women*, as Fatima had instructed him.

Age sixteen now, Laila had never felt so unsure of herself. She began to retreat again to the closet, to Amina's things. Like pretend-play, all the items spread out in the hallway, she re-created the world in which her mother might have lived: a land of opportunities, yes, but certainly not for someone like her. A young woman, bright and determined, not much older than Laila was then, naively hopeful about a country in which she was never quite at home. And how much like Laila Amina must have felt, if Fatima was all she, too, had.

Laila went to the album in the living room. She took out the picture of herself and Amina on the balcony, the week before the storm. In it, her mother looked worn and a little surprised at the moment the photo was taken. The two of them hugged, cheek to cheek, arms around one another. Laila touched her own face. She walked to the bathroom mirror: there, Amina's high and plump cheeks.

⌒

LAILA WAS SURE ABOUT one thing: when Fatima had something on her mind, she talked around it—testing the waters of Laila's receptiveness—until she came to the point. For days, Fatima inched toward a discussion about the storm.

"I've been wondering," she started, one afternoon. She folded her arms across her breasts. "Do you ever think about the hurricane?"

"Not the hurricane itself, no." Laila was equally circumspect, unsure of her aunty's intention. She held close the sadness she sometimes felt about Amina's absence.

"Do you think about your mum?"

"Once in a while. Why?"

"I'm just wondering." Fatima patted Laila's back and left it at that.

Three days passed before Fatima shared what she had been holding in, all the years since Amina's death. Laila was on the sofa when Fatima sat down next to her. She took the remote from the table, clicked off the television, and turned to Laila. Laila knew then that Fatima was ready to talk.

"I haven't slept through the night in years, thinking about the choice I made that day. I told Amina we would go get her after we finished boarding up the garage. That was the truth. But by the time we were done, I was famished. Rashid insisted that we pick you and Amina up first, because the closest restaurant that was open was fifteen minutes in the opposite direction of the French Market.

"*You don't know how traffic will be, coming back, if we go get food first,* he said.

"I was hungry and I argued him down. So we drove to get food. He was right about the traffic. It was almost at a standstill by the time we left the restaurant and headed toward the market. I saw that Amina had tried to reach me. By then, we couldn't make calls on our cells—the lines had gone dead. When we got to the stall, you and your mother were gone.

"Laila, I searched that entire market. A man told me he'd seen Amina get on a bus to the Superdome. Rashid and I packed up the boxes she'd left and we drove away. We heard on the radio that the dome was already full. The line of cars going that way was several miles long, the reporter said. We had a choice to make.

"*We could get stuck and not even make it inside the dome*, I said.

"Rashid, hands shaking on the steering wheel, drove in the other direction, away from the Superdome. It took almost ten hours for us to escape the path of the storm, but we made it. We found a motel near the Texas border and stayed there for a few days."

The quiet in the room swelled.

Laila moved to the edge of the sofa. "Is that everything?"

"That's it."

It was late. But neither of them had turned on the light.

"I don't know what to say."

"You don't have to say anything, Laila. I know it's a lot."

"All right," Laila nodded. "I'll see you in the morning."

Fatima sat, holding her face in her palms, until the dusk became black.

Once or twice, Laila had wondered why all of them hadn't been in the same place when the storm struck. But she had been too afraid to ask. She didn't want to know for certain that Aunty Fatima had been cruel to her mother. What she heard tonight was hard to forgive. Amina must have been frightened, knowing she and Laila had been left behind.

Laila decided for sure, then: she would move out of Fatima's house as soon as she turned eighteen.

IYANIFA: JOSEPH

Shells in the shape of shifting

THE ROOM COULD HAVE SWALLOWED HIM, WITH ITS cavernous ceiling and blinding morning light. Joseph lay on his back, hands behind his head, surrendered. Hours-old stubble cast a tint on his sleepy face.

After the storm, his mornings changed. In place of the rote sequence that once prepared him for driving, he woke up slowly, wrote down a goal for the day, and eased into his calisthenics on the balcony while coffee brewed on the stove.

Joseph had become an easier-going man—less obsessed with the ramblings in his mind and more curious about where life might lead. Now in his sixties, he was still fit. Three times a week for the past nine years, he'd practiced bodyweight exercises. And because he drank a lot of water and soaked in the sun when he could, his aura sparkled good health. Joseph could hardly believe it; these had become the best days of his life.

Last night, out of nowhere it seemed, Joseph craved home— back home. He had been away for twenty-eight years and felt unrooted. America would never embrace him like the soil of Yorubaland—the comfort of his family village, where he was known by all of his names. We say in our culture that the place of one's birth is curated to the needs of the body; its air, water, and land are remedial for the ailments of the foreign-gone. Sooner or later, they must return.

Joseph had wanted a family. The desire had not gone away with time. Instead, he managed it by learning to make friends. *My life is full in other ways*, he would reassure anyone who was concerned that he might be lonely. Once he turned sixty, the offers to set him up on dates stopped. A couple of buddies encouraged him to find an older woman—but one younger than him—who already had children. Joseph was not interested.

With George and Rashid years gone, Fatima and Laila all the way in the San Francisco Bay Area, Joseph's old life—his old haunts, his old habits—were ghosts of the past. Sure, there were a few friends he kept up with on social media, but seeing photos of them walking their children down the aisle and taking their grandbabies for ice cream, Joseph felt like an outcast.

ABOUT FOUR YEARS AFTER the hurricane, Joseph's mother had died. It took six days for his sister to reach him with the news. "We have all agreed you do not need to bother coming. Just send us the money," she'd said, before Joseph could speak at all.

"The money for what, what do you mean?" he had asked, knowing already what she meant, but being incredulous still, and needing her to say it aloud.

And then she did, and Joseph was not the same, for a very long while. "Where have you been all this time?" she had asked. "What dreams have you made come true while your mother suffered?" The monthly allowance he had been sending wasn't enough to cover his mother's living expenses, his sister said. Besides, his siblings resented his absence. He was in America being free while they had stayed and taken care of their mother.

Joseph sent the money: enough for the funeral expenses and her preceding hospital stay. He left the celebration of life costs to them. His sadness at losing his mother was compounded by anger at his siblings and shame that he hadn't become enough.

In her last letter to him: *Don't worry, Joseph,* she had written. *You are a good man and a good son, success or not.* Those words made him feel worse. Inadvertently, she had confirmed his darkest thoughts.

⁓

LURKING UNDERNEATH JOSEPH'S LONGING for home was his wondering about Laila. A toddler the last time he saw her, she would be an adult now, he thought. Through the Nigerian transatlantic gossip stream, he'd heard that Esther and Fatima were estranged. That was not a surprise, in light of Amina's death. Still, it was a shame that Laila and Esther did not know one another. Laila. Sixteen years of thinking of someone every day, and yet living like they don't exist. And although he did not want to remember it, he owed Esther the story of what had happened to Amina in the dome. He sat up on the edge of the bed and wrote down the day's goal: *Call Fatima.*

After a shower as cold as his body could stand—a feature of his new wellness plan—Joseph got dressed and walked the two miles to Oshun Coffee.

"Fatima, long time," he said when she answered the phone. Joseph had not fully formed why he was calling or what he would say.

He and Fatima talked longer than he had planned, and about many things—some meaningful, some trivial.

She had opened a boutique, and Rashid had remarried, she said. A woman much younger than Fatima. "He's such a cliché, that man." Then she asked if Joseph had finally returned home.

She still hadn't, she confessed, with life always happening, all of the time.

"That's why I called, actually. I'm thinking of going back in a few months," Joseph said. "Maybe to stay for a while, take care of some business with my mum's property."

And then they reached Laila.

"She moved out a few months ago," Fatima said.

Laila worked part-time at her boutique, Fatima explained, so she still saw the girl. The coldness in her voice kept Joseph from asking more. He hoped Laila was getting settled okay in her new place, he offered.

Fatima was quiet. So Joseph shared the thought that had come to him.

"If it's all right with you, I'd like Laila to go with me, for two or three weeks. It's been on my mind. I think it will be good for her to meet her grandmother. You know, make a connection back to her family."

"Nigeria?" Fatima shook her head, though Joseph couldn't see. "She's never been out of the country, Joseph."

"I understand." Joseph softened his voice, to reassure her. "I'll handle everything. Her ticket, hotel, and of course I'll have a car to take her around. She'll be safe."

"I'm her family."

"I know you are. And the trip won't change that in any way."

Fatima sighed. Joseph held his breath.

"Is this about Laila, or is it really about you and Esther?"

Joseph admired Fatima's bluntness—he always had. "If I'm being honest, both. Going home feels like what I'm supposed to do. That's the only way I can put it." Too, he was haunted by his withholding of Amina's final moments from Esther.

"Let me think about it. I'll bring it up with Laila and see what she says. Then you can ask her yourself."

"I would appreciate that very much. Thank you, Fatima."

Joseph clicked off. He was thrilled!

The call—even while he still waited on Laila's answer—made him excited about returning to Nigeria. He was already thinking about seeing Esther. He had asked around discreetly, and hadn't heard any rumors that she was involved with anyone. If Joseph was ever going to have his chance, this would be it.

He tipped his head and tossed back the last of his now-cold cappuccino. He jogged home, eager to plan the trip.

IYANIFA: LAILA

Shells in the shape of judgment

IN HER NEW APARTMENT, LAILA WAS SURROUNDED BY these things: the born-again couple on the left, the poodle-haired property manager in the front, and all around, the feeling that this wouldn't end well. She knew this the first time she'd turned onto the street. Even in the shine of a sunny day, the agitating voice inside her cast a gray sluggishness on everything in motion—like feet dragging. Her mind went to soothing itself: however long she'd felt adrift, she could make a home wherever she went.

Laila had made good on her plan—almost. Two weeks after she turned nineteen, she'd moved out on her own. Partly by working for Fatima, part babysitting, part hoarding her allowance the last three years, she had saved enough for first-last-and-deposit on an apartment that was admittedly in one of the shadier parts of town. And though Aunty Fatima had to co-sign the lease, this was Laila's place, fully.

Her new apartment, tiny as it was, sat in a lush and admirable did-it-on-one's-own garden with birds of paradise and succulents of varied plumpness. Tucked greenly away from the city's failings, this was somewhere you'd live because you chose it.

Laila had been shocked by the low listing price online. Aunty Fatima had been concerned that there was an ulterior motive—a lure for human trafficking, possibly—and had run a full background check on the property and owner before she and Laila went to take a look.

"Do you really like it?" From the apartment's living room, Fatima could see the kitchen, bathroom, and closet-size bedroom.

The place was very small but cute and well-furnished—perfect for someone like her who was just starting out, Laila thought. "I love it!"

Laila was beaming, Fatima couldn't deny that. And she would be living just five minutes from home. Fatima liked that. She suppressed the urge to smile and told the owner they would take it. But because this was Laila's first apartment, they would sign a six-month lease, and see how things go, she said. Now, Laila had been at the apartment a full four months and would have to decide soon if she wanted to stay.

When Laila met her, the poodle-haired property manager, short and yoga-built, moved with the swiftness of someone both proud and angry to go it alone. She was busy, busy, busy. Always under the gun, just hanging in there, and having to check her schedule before agreeing to anything. Fifteen years after the divorce, the ex-husband was still an asshole, she told Laila. She sometimes watched the evening news hoping it was he that had been mowed down by the drunk driver. She couldn't wait for their last-born to turn eighteen.

Laila nodded.

"Let me know if you need anything?" An offer that sounded like a threat.

Laila imagined her new life, running into this poodle-haired woman in the shared yard, the discomfort of trying to avoid pesky small talk. She worried about her persisting weakness: an inability to escape the lurking dark, these many years on. The agitating voice that would return and insist everything was a threat.

⁓

LAILA NEEDED HER NEW LIFE, living alone, to work out; she needed Aunty Fatima to see that she could do it. That morning, the ten-minute walk to the coffee shop made her aware of her legs. Something had changed in her gait. Something slight, not quite a limp, but perhaps the beginning of one. In her uncertainty, she had slowed down.

The streets were empty, but she wasn't alone. The sidewalk was a plank, and this walk an epic pronouncement. If things went on to get better, if she could beat the voice this time, then this place, gray and deserted as it was, could be the means and not the end. If things didn't get better, then this place, gray and deserted as it was, was in fact the end. The spattering of clouds had become faces, and the sidewalk the table around which they gathered and judged.

"I have a small soy latte on the bar. Thanks darlin'." The barista said it in that sing-song way that was so rehearsed, it was clear the gesture was not about Laila or the drink, but about the coins and the occasional bills that might meet the bottom of his tip jar, every fourth customer if he was lucky. He smiled, and Laila reached for the paper cup.

Maybe—no, if only—he cared that she was there. But he avoided her eyes. His sing-song, she was sure then, was just the practiced finesse of the coffee shop hipster who worked this job and another or two to make fraying ends meet.

Laila held the cup to her chest and walked toward the floor-length windows. There sat a young man. His laptop was open to a spreadsheet flush with numbers. A stack of papers and two colored pencils sat at his right hand. He looked up and scanned the room, hoping to be distracted from the mountain of work. Laila, this day, was willing. Passing all the other open seats, she chose the stool right next to him.

They were friendly, immediately. Both had roots in Nigeria, they discovered.

"And mums, is she here in the States?" the young man asked.

"No, she was. But not anymore. It's been years—"

"Oh okay, she's back in Nigeria?"

"Yeah, there." Laila rubbed the back of her neck. She lied because it was easier.

"Right, so you're still schooling then?"

"Yeah, just starting." She lied again because this, too, was easier. Aunty Fatima wanted her to go to college, but Laila was unsure.

"Are you going back, after?"

"Nigeria? I don't know. Not now. Soon, though." Laila shrugged too casually for this to be true. "I'll be here a while until I figure things out."

This scene recurred every few weeks: meeting a random but familiar-feeling someone who was also Nigerian, and who, until recently, had not been home in years. And now that he had, he must recruit others to do the same.

"Man, the poverty is craaazy in some parts," the young man said, as if he'd merely been a tourist. "We think Black Americans have it bad? I mean, this isn't poor-with-bootleg-cable-TV poor. This is poor like no-toilet-paper-or-indoor-toilet poor. You know what I mean?"

Laila laughed, to appear invested.

She did not know what he meant, but she listened to this story and others like it because she remembered Fatima telling her something similar: How she would rinse her crotch with a small bowl of cool, cloudy water. Her legs spread across the cluttered gutter that ran to the back of her childhood home. Or she would squat on the wide, curved steps leading into a concrete hole—the shalanga where everyone else had squatted and dumped for years. *You spread, rub, and rinse at the same time*, Fatima had said. Cold air would weave between her legs as she rose against the drip. Wet, but not enough to soak her pants. That was how it was done, Fatima had explained.

"Craaazy," Laila said, mimicking the young man's disbelief. Nothing more.

The young man squinted, waiting for something else to suggest she'd really understood.

But Laila was too self-conscious about her legitimacy as African to admit that she actually hadn't been to Nigeria. That although both of her parents were from there, she just had not been. That her mother had died when she was a toddler, and no one would talk about her father, George. That she had been raised by her Aunty Fatima, who had no interest in going home after divorcing Uncle Rashid. All of this was much too much to tell a stranger just passing time.

When she reached the bottom of her latte, she introduced herself: "Laila."

"Tosin," the young man said. He stood to pack up his things, work unfinished. He wrote his phone number on a napkin. "If you ever wanna talk about home," he said.

⁓

"ABI, LISTEN TO MISS AMERICANA!" one of Fatima's California relatives had said when Laila tried to speak the Yoruba she knew. "Ehn, maybe you can teach us to twist our tongues and wrinkle our noses too." In between hoarse laughter, they had managed to reveal their grievance: Laila's Yoruba was watered down, her intonations westernized. She didn't know the language, so of course she couldn't know the culture.

Hence, for awkward diasporans, the stories of home are shared mostly in passing, between strangers who dare not say when they had last been, or, in Laila's case, that they hadn't been at all. And should they admit this, or that they, too, can't name the current Nigerian president, or the country's latest dance craze, they risk the gates of authenticity—guarded by those upon whom true Nigerianness is supernaturally conferred—being shut against them forevermore.

Laila walked to the bar and ordered another coffee.

She looked at her phone: a missed call from Aunty Fatima.

"You never pick up, do you?" Fatima began, in her voicemail. "I told Joseph you would think about it. It's your choice if you want to go to Nigeria with him," she said, in the middle of a message that started with an inventory of what she had been up to over the weekend at the boutique, and ended with, god willing, she hoped Laila was finally making friends.

"Nigeria?" Laila looked at the napkin on the table: Tosin's number, written in colored-pencil green. She hoped this was a sign.

On her way back home from the coffee shop, pedestrians made tense, ruthless gestures. A baby stroller knocked into her ankle and the woman pushing it rolled her eyes at Laila, as though her leg were some twig on an otherwise clear path. Drivers sped up as she stepped into the crosswalk. Yet this walk to the apartment seemed new. On her way out, she had felt forsaken; returning, her life was on the verge. The sun, too, seemed pleased with its sky.

⌐

JOSEPH CALLED HER the following day.

"Laila!" he said, as soon as she answered, like they were old friends.

And though Laila had planned to be reserved, wanting to appear as if she had more going on in her life than this call, she couldn't help the cheery "Joseph!" in return.

Joseph told her that while he and Laila had never met in New Orleans, he knew her mother, Amina. Then he told her the story of the doll. That in photos he used to see on Rashid's desk at the garage, Laila had thick, big curls just like that doll.

"I still have it, somewhere," Laila said, pretending to be unsure. In fact, the doll was in her new bedroom, on her bed. She could touch and hold it, a reminder from the short time she had been with Amina.

"I'm sure you miss your mum," Joseph said. "That's not easy."

Laila did not know what to say but "Thank you."

And then, the main reason for his call: Nigeria.

How did Laila feel about going? Joseph asked.

She'd been thinking about it since Fatima brought it up, she said. She wanted to meet her grandmother—anyone from her mother's family, really. She had so many questions Aunty Fatima couldn't answer. "Or maybe she doesn't want to, I don't know," Laila said—this time, truly unsure.

"I think this trip will be good for everyone, I really do," Joseph said.

They talked about the timeline. Joseph had found good tickets available for travel two months from then. He would go first, about a week ahead of Laila. When she arrived, he'd pick her up at the airport—Murtala International. The custom of such a visit is that Laila would stay with a family member, but given the circumstances, Joseph thought she might be more comfortable at a hotel. "What do you think?"

Laila wasn't often asked about her thoughts. She felt happy—she was sure of it—and that meant something. "Your plan sounds great," she said.

"Good." Of course, they would talk again before the trip. And she could call him with anything that was on her mind, Joseph told her.

After they hung up, Laila sat at her kitchen table and replayed the call in her head. "It's really true," she said aloud. Her life was happening! Finally, she might see where and how her mother had lived. And she hadn't had to struggle for it, as Aunty Fatima had insisted would be the case. "Sometimes life does arrive on a gilded plate."

WITH NO NEW EFFORT, Laila's strides became less pinched.

The poodle-haired manager scuttled about her garden. The tomatoes would need replanting, she insisted. She couldn't stand those who made it through life too easily. Cheeriness annoyed her, but more than that, she hated contentedness. And she hated Laila for that reason—she didn't seem to have earned all the years of her age, because if she was burdened, it didn't show. She walked with the litheness of someone freer than she ought to have been. How can you trust someone that never complains? You can't.

It had not become any easier to know what makes a place home. Laila had had the feeling once, when she was little—when she and Aunty Fatima had just moved to California. She'd been buoyed, plainly certain Fatima would always be there. This was before the boyfriends Fatima brought home, and the disapproving voice in Laila's head. But here, in this apartment that she'd chosen, even with the chirps of birds and the squeals of toddlers, sadness crept.

And then Joseph, in that one call, had offered Laila more to anticipate than she'd ever had. This place, this time might not be bad after all. Laila's world—living alone in relative ease, having a chance to go to college—would have been beyond Amina's reach. She owed it to her mother, to Aunty Fatima, and perhaps even to Esther and Joseph now, to become someone they could point to, proud.

Laila opened her apartment door and sat on the steps that led into the garden. Something in her peeked through. A feeling lit up by the decidedness of a peppermint leaf pushing through the cement. If she had seen it before, it looked new now—the depth of the blade, the green gloss of the leaf. To her right, the black tulip magnolia, dangling its drooping, purplish blooms, swayed in the evening wind.

ESTHER

Shells in the shape of spring

AMINA.

Who are these people that make pronouncements? They tell us our lives will be blessed and we rejoice; when they say there is calamity around the corner, we despair. We go years hoping for the one good thing, and another many years lamenting our setbacks. Our pursuits depend on which oracle or prophet has had their say. As for me, I have given it up, the malady of good fortune.

I ran the restaurant and made my money. I took care of myself without input from anyone. I told your father's kin to leave me alone. They must have been glad to see my suffering. I deserved what came to me, they might have said. Well, wouldn't Sani feel the loss too? Or is the death of a child a woman's alone to endure?

Then, the talkers. Right after the storm, their words were kind—the whole town was concerned. After you died, they brought their condolences and cries of sorrow. At first the neighbors visited with food. When they did not receive the customary gratitude from me, they stopped coming altogether. I kept to myself as the years passed. Soon, their restraint dissolved:

"She's lost her mind," I heard said.

"She needs to move on," they decided.

"Move on with what? She has nothing to live for. Who can blame her?"

I agree with them that I cannot be blamed. We have dreams for the future, then destiny has its say. I accept the outlay of the shells I was dealt.

⌣

THEN JOSEPH RANG ME. I hadn't imagined his voice over the telephone, or any medium for that matter. And now that he was old like me, its tone was even more of a surprise. He had taken my number from Fatima, he said. Fatima. Over the years, she'd sent letters with pictures of Laila tucked between the pages. I could not respond. She and Rashid left you alone to defend yourself against a storm, Amina. I cannot forgive it.

But you must know I prayed for Laila every day; of course I did. I am the part of her that lives. The shame of the years passing made it harder and harder to call Fatima and ask about my granddaughter.

When can I see her?

How is she growing?

Does she miss her mother?

I asked these questions, only to myself. Then Fatima stopped writing.

"Esther," Joseph said, in his old-man voice. I knew it was him before he even said, "It's Joseph."

He had talked to Laila.

"Laila? My granddaughter."

That's right, he said. "She wants to visit."

"Me? Here? Come to Nigeria?"

That was also right. "I think it's time you meet Amina's daughter."

I could not believe it, Amina. I did not think I could be happy again.

"When will you come?"

"I'm working on everything. In two months, I hope. I will let you know. Esther?"

"Yes."

"It's time for you to meet your granddaughter."

I understood why he said it twice: regret can keep you turning back.

IYANIFA: LAILA

Shells in the shape of air

LAILA FIRST HEARD THE BREATH IN A DREAM. IN IT, SHE walks into a room that is empty except for a bed against the wall, a fan by the window, and the low, smooth breath that fills each of these objects with sound. This—the breath of her mother, which has led her to places that exhale on their own—leaves a mark like pencil lead engraved into a wooden grade-school desk: *Amina was here.*

These days, Laila goes to cafés because the things in them breathe: the chocolate scent of the coffee beans; the people and their focused movements; the acoustic-heavy music. And though she thinks she finds the breath here, she is the one who carries it. From the dream, it pierces her skin. And she remembers her mother.

THE FEAR OF WANTING to become something but never quite being it had, for the last year, kept Laila awake into the mornings. Aunty Fatima had urged her to apply to community college when she returned from Nigeria, and Laila had said she would consider it, but that was just to keep Fatima from bringing it up again and again. Under the weight of expectation, she clung to these: the breathing sanctuary of the neighborhood café and the nightly images it provoked. The room, the bed, the fan, and their pulse felt something like *artist*—what she hoped to someday be.

⁓

TODAY, LIKE THE ONES BEFORE, it was the same: small soy latte. "See you tomorrow," Laila rhymed to the barista's sing-song. It was silly she'd said that, she realized, because this morning she was not at the neighborhood coffee shop, but at a generic stand at the San Francisco International Airport, on her way to Nigeria. "It's the practiced finesse," she said to herself, remembering the barista from her favorite café.

Joseph had sent a text message last night, to make sure she was ready for the trip. He reminded her to put a fake address on the disembarkation card, to avoid being followed and robbed by airline workers who targeted Nigerians from America. Oh, and he had something to give her, he said. If she wanted it, she could have it. *Amina is your mother after all*, he wrote. *But I'm also thinking . . . Esther.*

Joseph didn't have to say more than that. Laila replied that she understood. She had something, too, but would wait to tell Joseph. Fatima had given her the leather bag of Amina's belongings when she moved into her own apartment. Laila collected the envelopes with *Esther* written on the front and put them in her purse. She couldn't go to Nigeria empty-handed.

This must be joy, Laila thought. Tucked in the back corner of an airport coffee shop, she stared out the window, craving some Blackness—her senses longing for a place to fit. She thought of Tosin and his seriousness about returning home. A gray-haired woman in a floral dress walked by, pulling a suitcase at her side. And it made Laila want to cry, this stranger looking back, holding her eyes with a smile—a face she had never seen, which could be her mother's, and which she already missed.

IYANIFA: JOSEPH AND LAILA

Shells in the shape of souls

IN HEAVEN OR ON EARTH, LIFE FULFILLS ITS DEEPEST
longing—the reunion of souls who have come by way of providence. The shells tell me so.

⁓

FROM THE INSTANT they heard each other's voice, Joseph
and Laila felt like the family the other had sought. Laila would
never call him *baba, uncle,* or even *grandpa.* In her thoughts,
warmly, she called him *the old man.* In his timely appearance;
his gentleness with words; his understanding, without her having to say much—could they have been kin, she wondered, in
another life?

And the moment they saw one another, it was confirmed.
Their mutual liking was immediate and inexplicable, as with
souls between whom goodness has transpired.

Joseph waited behind the customs gate. Laila spotted him
easily, not just because she had seen pictures; he looked like
what *father* might be. And that is true: in a handful of lifetimes,
Laila had been Joseph's daughter. They will forever find each
other again.

Laila put her bags aside and Joseph opened his arms to hug her. The tightness in her head dissolved. In her nineteen years, for once she felt she deserved this new and strange happiness. Joseph, who had all but given up on ever having a family, understood then that blessings take the time they take—destiny does not hurry.

IYANIFA: ESTHER AND JOSEPH

Shells in the shape of desire

IN HER LETTERS TO AMINA, ESTHER HAD BEGUN WITH
Joseph. She heard through the transatlantic gossip stream that
he had moved to New Orleans. Life having drained her of
the will for love, she would never ask Amina about him. But
Joseph never forgot her. He has spent lifetimes chasing Esther.
This part of their story will be bittersweet. The shells tell me so.

⁓

IT HAD BEEN LIKE a thousand years, the multitude of lives
and places between Esther and Joseph since they first met.
They had walked paths apart, only to return to the threshold
where an opening to love first swung. The hard years moved
them well into their sixties, more subdued—an era of old age
in which they could say and do as they pleased. It was a relief,
too, not expecting another to resurrect dead dreams. Joseph
and Esther could take things just as they were.

When Joseph first asked, Esther said no, she would prefer
that he didn't come with Laila to meet her—not initially. She
would send her driver to pick up the girl instead.

But he insisted.

And Esther couldn't find a reason not to see him right away, other than her vanity. He was about her age, if she remembered right—and she was sure she did. But she'd lost the chance for him to see her again the way he had, that first time. A part of her wanted him to wonder what she might have become, rather than knowing for sure. However young a woman looked or felt for her age, she'd been told, something on her body betrayed the passage of time.

But Joseph was old too, wasn't he? Whichever parts had fallen from their proper places on her were similarly drooped on him. She giggled, remembering the comedian who described an old man's testicles over a commode as teabags dipped into a cup of water. "Men have no place to talk," Esther said aloud. "Age is just as unkind to them."

⁓

JOSEPH HAD STOPPED EXPECTING life to change, as if newness would just fall from the sky. He knew now that god didn't work that way. Imagining Esther's loss had been hard for him. Amina's body had never been found. He could only believe that after the guards picked her up, despite appearing to have a place for her, they had tossed her aside, as if she was unworthy of being preserved.

Unaccounted for. Would it have been different if she had been an American, if she had been white? When they saw her ankara head tie, what nasty things about Africans did they joke about among themselves? Perhaps something about her civilization or her ability to speak English—ignorant shit like that. He was still angry; this much, Joseph knew.

And he was sure he could have done more. Nothing had eased this singular guilt. Certainly not drinking until he passed out, trying to forget, as he'd done in the earlier years. With time, he became better at lining up the questions he could have asked the officials in the dome that day. He remembered the face of the nurse that had come for Amina. But he hadn't searched for her after he left the dome. The shame of his silence kept him from telling Rashid and Fatima that he'd seen Amina there. Not until he called Fatima about Laila, sixteen years later, did he finally confess it.

Fatima had been kinder than Joseph could accept. *I understand*, had been her response when he explained the reasons for his silence all that time. They talked and then they were quiet. In the things unsaid, Joseph found consolation for his shortcomings; it wasn't too late, after all, for him to begin again.

⌒

SOMETIMES, THE END IS suspected from the beginning. When Amina walked away from Esther's flat that last time, her feet hadn't left a hint of a print in the dust. Esther allows herself to remember it now because the scab of the pain has finally flaked. What remains is tender, but able to withstand.

She read once that children do not belong to their parents, but come through them to fulfill their own destinies, dreams to which parents are not privy. This was said, of course, by a man poet. *Who am I now, without a child to call me Mummy?* Esther wondered. She would soon be called a new name.

For welcoming Joseph and Laila, there would be a preparation in three parts: first, the time and place; second, the food; and third, Esther herself. Morning was the easiest time of day. Fresh from dreaming, optimism infused the air. Home would have been the traditional place to welcome Joseph and Laila, but hers was a vault weighted with grief. She had kept Amina's things, trying to preserve her presence, and though she'd moved to a new home, even there the dust of years remained. It would be the restaurant, then. She'd fill the room with vases of flowers—fake ones in water, to make it all look real.

Food, though, worried her. What does an American girl eat? From the internet videos and the stories she had heard, not the solid and grounding food on which Amina grew. It could be that Joseph, too, had forgotten the taste of his youth. Would he flinch now at jollof rice and dodo, at moin moin and gari? In the end, she would make the things she made best. No one seasoned food like Esther; gift and art, rather than practice, were how that came to be.

And then there was herself. It had been a long time since Esther had asked her body to make more than the barest effort. She would have to consult at the beauty shop to see what was needed. Plaits with some attachments would do just fine, she thought. She was prepared to ignore the pushy salon girls who encouraged a dye and wax each time she went, as they picked at her roots and rubbed her brows. "A manicure and pedicure are enough," she had always responded, defensive.

But beneath all that, Esther's heart might have leapt a time or two. Here she was, preparing everything for Joseph! Love, after this long time? Esther had to manage her excitement while out—lest the talkers talk—because in every moment since Joseph had called, she'd wanted to scream for joy.

⌒

HERE JOSEPH WAS. At home, but no longer at ease. He visited his childhood haunts; he dressed similarly to the men his age; he joked cleverly and slapped hands to show he was just like them. But everyone—at the gas station, in the supermarket, on the side of the road—recognized he wasn't one of them. And they let him know it. They would smirk into the air and then say some words to the side of their face, lips pursed, under their breath. Just at the tip of derision, to remind Joseph that he wasn't welcomed home.

Relating to his siblings wasn't any easier. His sister had invited him to a family party on his second night home. He thought she was ready to make amends over their falling out after their mother's death. But when Joseph arrived, he might as well have been walking into the arctic—the coldness that awaited him in each room. The few relatives who did talk to him ended the conversation by asking for something from America. "I would love a Rolex. Can you send me one?" a cousin asked, the way one might ask to be mailed a postcard from abroad.

When Joseph said, "Ah, sorry. I don't think I can afford that," the cousin sucked his teeth and shrugged. He walked away before Joseph could explain further, and Joseph sat alone outside the rest of his time there. He left the party weary, questioning whether Nigeria could ever feel like home again.

⌣

JOSEPH PROMISED TO TAKE Laila to all the places Amina had lived, throughout Ibadan. Her hotel was a twenty-minute drive from his ancestral home, where he'd spent many of his holidays as a boy, and where he was staying now. Each early morning, after his coffee and workout in the compound, he picked up Laila. They drove around, Joseph playing tour guide, stopping for food or pulling over on the side of the road so she could take a photo or video. These young ones, he noticed, liked to document everything.

He waited to hear whether it could be arranged for Laila to visit Oyin or her grandfather, Sani—the one person whose whereabouts no one seemed to know. When nothing came forth—Oyin was out of the country on business, her assistant said—Joseph planned his own itinerary for Laila, interspersing her requests with visits to Yoruba landmarks.

Most of all, he was eager for her to meet Esther. Joseph himself had not yet seen Esther since arriving in Nigeria last week. He was ready and a little afraid. When they'd talked last, Esther agreed that he would come to her first, alone. Laila and Esther would meet after that. Joseph decided he would take the chance to tell Esther about Amina's last moments.

And now, the day had arrived.

⌢

THE OUTSIDE OF ESTHER'S RESTAURANT was not at all what Joseph had imagined. Light pink and yellow, it sat at the bottom of a two-story building shared with a lawyer's office. A walk up the front stairs led to a doorway with neon-lit writing: *Esther's Palace*.

Joseph stood at the door. He felt seventeen again, the butterflies clawing at his belly. Would the inexplicable rush through his body still be there? He was anxious to feel it, like the first time.

He pulled the metal handle and walked inside.

The strangeness they had feared did not happen. Joseph, still with his luminous smile, came immediately toward Esther as he walked into the restaurant. They hugged arms and shoulders, unsure where else to hold.

"You look well, wow," Joseph said. It was true. He could not remember now the Esther of their youth; the face before him was lovelier. He wanted to touch her again. He had been trying to get back here—through America, through Maryam, through the possibilities that never materialized—to Esther.

"Ah." Esther's confidence soared. "Could you have expected otherwise?"

Joseph laughed. His shoulders came down, at ease now and thankful for her gentle teasing.

And then they talked—more sincerely than either had anticipated. About how they hadn't really known each other, those years ago; how despite that one day at the restaurant with Sani, they were still like strangers. It is easy to make more of a passing moment than it really was, they agreed.

"Except we don't seem to be doing that." He looked up at Esther, hoping for something to affirm his feeling.

"Maybe."

Joseph laughed, this time because he had more saved up than he was ready to say. If the time came, and Esther gave him the chance, he would tell her that he had loved her from the moment he saw her, walking the dirt road home. And if she wanted him, he would find a way for them to be together—here or in America.

Esther looked at his hands. She knew, of course, that he had driven a taxi, but just observing them, it was hard to place the kind of work they must have done—they looked worn yet soft. "I know you brought something in that bag." Just in noticing, she wanted to cry.

Joseph coughed, then pulled his knees to stop their shaking. He didn't know where to begin. "I saw Amina at the Super-dome." He rubbed his tongue over his teeth. "We were in the same section, on the field. Maybe about thirty or so feet apart. She didn't know I was there. I was sure we would see each other again, at another time."

Esther's long breath filled the pause. In Joseph's conversation with Fatima, they had agreed he would tell Esther the full truth. But looking at her now, he had to decide anew.

"I walked around the dome as much as I could, trying to steady my mind. I didn't see Amina or Laila for quite some time. I had no reason to think anything was wrong. At some point, I fell asleep again on the field. And then I heard crying." Joseph bowed his head, describing what he saw when he reached the hall. "I was there, before they took her away." At first, he lingered behind the certainty of what he knew. He walked his words over and around the hardest part: that she might have already died, even before they moved her body. "I was beside her, at the end. I thought about you. I held her for you, Esther. I told her what you might have wanted to say: that you were so proud of her, that you were there too." He reached into the canvas satchel, pulled out the plastic bag, and placed it in Esther's hands. "I found this later."

Esther untied the bag's handles and rubbed the ankara wrap. "This was one of the ones she wanted to take, when she left. One of mine." The lightness of it, the waxed exterior having been long worn, revealed its many washings. Had Amina done so by hand or machine? The patterns shined, still.

"I've never washed it," Joseph said.

Esther kept the cloth in her lap. What she wanted to do was hold it to her nose, close her eyes, and inhale as deeply as her lungs would allow. She wanted to put it under a bright light and search it for a thread of hair, anything that might remain. Could something still be there, these many years later? Maybe a scent that belonged only to her daughter—for the essence of a person lingers in their things, it is said, even after they've gone.

But because Joseph was there watching her, and because it would hurt too much to find out in front of him that the cloth had nothing left of Amina but its having been at her last breath, she let it stay in her lap and patted it again.

Joseph pried her fingers from the cloth and held her hand. She made her wrist stubborn, unwilling. He squeezed it tighter still. Then Esther began to cry; the soundless tears of a woman tired of a life that had yet to treat her kindly. Perhaps it was the grace of him anticipating her need or it was just the need being filled, but Esther felt something quiet, maybe like peace. And if, from then on, it happened that life gave her nothing more to hope for, she could bear having to accept that Amina was really gone.

Joseph rubbed Esther's cheek. She let her tears run down his hand. Neither spoke, right then.

IYANIFA: OYIN AND ESTHER

Shells in the shape of peace

THE ONE WHO HAD BEEN REJECTED SHALL NOW BE THE cornerstone, their acceptable religion says. Well, in Ifa it is the same. Oyin, the child born of deception, the one whose mother made her an orphan, the sister whose birthright was stolen, surprised everybody—the ones on earth, at least—when she became the rock on which Esther leaned after Amina died.

Every day since, Oyin has replayed the last words she said to her sister. Almost twenty years after their fight, she thinks she is the one who cursed Amina; she thinks she called her death forth.

⌒

NEWS OF THE STORM came while Oyin was in the back office of her salon, eating lunch and playing a game on her phone. The afternoon radio newscaster, the one with the dull voice, had said thousands were feared dead or missing in a New Orleans hurricane that was one of the most devastating in US history. She knew it as soon as she heard those words: Amina was dead. It was a feeling, as certain as the day. Now she would have to get to Esther before she heard the news from elsewhere. Oyin's driver sped them down the road to the restaurant as quickly as traffic would allow.

When they arrived, the head waitress told them Esther had already left. "She has heard the news, Oyin. Everybody has." Coming from the kitchen, Oyin could hear the drab recitation of that same news anchor.

Nearly thirty thousand were stuck in the Louisiana Superdome, he said, and the situation inside was horrific—worse than anything thoughts could conceive. People were exhausted, losing patience and their minds. Officials were being blamed, from the city's mayor to the nation's president. "George Bush doesn't care about Black people," one American rapper had said.

Oyin walked to a booth to sit and arrange her thoughts. She must remain steady and hopeful. For herself and for Esther, who would certainly need that in the days ahead. Sani came to mind, and Oyin picked up her phone to call. They had not spoken in months. His presence, now, could send Esther over the edge, she decided. Whatever else was coming, Oyin wouldn't be the cause of more pain. She would go home, pack a few things, then go to Esther's and wait to hear from Fatima and Rashid—and maybe by some miracle of god, Amina too. The drive to Esther's house was longer than it had ever been.

⌒

WHEN RASHID'S AND FATIMA'S PARENTS came to Esther's gate several days later, Oyin was the one who went to greet them.

"Is she dead?" she asked flatly, to prepare then and there how to tell it to Esther.

"They have not found her body, but they believe she is gone, yes," Fatima's father said. And while the entrance of the house was too far from the gate for Esther to hear anything, standing at the door that led to the kitchen, she began to wail. Hands on her head, twisting her whole body, a pulling-of-the-hair kind of lamentation.

Oyin ran and grabbed Esther by the waist.

"Mummy, please, let's go inside. We'll sit down, get you some water. You haven't slept in so long. And you're tired, aren't you? Yes, I know. When you wake up, we can talk. It's okay. Let's go."

Rashid's and Fatima's parents stood, gawking. Oyin, with one arm around the shoulders of an Esther who had begrudgingly agreed to go inside—for water at least—waved the family away behind her back. The gateman, understanding everything without being told, ushered the parents out of the compound.

⌒

OVER THE FOLLOWING WEEKS, the news that flowed in about Amina—her whereabouts before the storm, her ordeal during it, and her missing body after—was heavy. And it was Oyin who shouldered it, calling officials in the US and sifting through the scantest pieces of information. In the downtime when no news came, she kept Esther busy with card games, new snacks, trash television, and stories of the years she and Amina lived together under Esther's roof.

"Did you ever find out what happened with the Volks?" she asked one afternoon.

"Which Volks—my white one?"

"Yes, the white one. Your first car."

"What do you mean, what happened to it?"

"The morning you woke up and found all that shit inside." Oyin could not get the word *shit* out without laughing. And that was when Esther understood.

"So it was you!"

"Well, it wasn't me alone. Amina planned it, but I helped her—with all the dumping." Oyin told her the story, from beginning to end.

Esther couldn't pretend to be angry, even if she tried. She felt inexplicable pride at the two girls hiding this one deed from her for so many years. She could not believe that she hadn't sussed out their plan. What she did find out, years later, and what she would never tell Oyin, is that Niyi had also been intimate with Amina, which meant her daughter certainly knew what *sweet banana* was, all the way back then.

The two women could laugh now about a past that had at times been unbearable for them both. And when they remembered Amina again, they wept. She would never return to them, except in memory.

"She was my sister, Amina."

"Which means you are my daughter."

The shells told this, too: Oyin and Esther—through Temi, through Amina—were meant to be kin.

⁓

A MONTH AGO, Esther went to Oyin's salon to tell her she had news. This time, it was good—Oyin could tell, before Esther said anything, because of the lightness in her feet. Joseph was coming back to Nigeria and bringing Laila with him, she said. Esther and Oyin were going to meet Laila, after all these years.

"Amina's daughter, my niece!" Oyin couldn't believe it.

Esther would see Joseph first, she had decided. Then they could all get together. But after her meeting with Joseph, she called Oyin and said they needed to talk. Oyin, just returning from a business trip, went to Esther's Palace straight from the airport.

"There's something that has been weighing on me, for decades," Esther began.

Oyin's body tensed.

"You know, as the firstborn, our culture says there are certain things you are entitled to."

"Right, I understand."

"I don't think you do." Esther shook her head. "You see, a few years before Amina left for America, I went to ask Iyanifa when Amina would get married."

"I remember." Oyin felt sharpness in her chest and tried to talk over it, to avoid the widening sensation.

But Esther was determined to get the words out. Iyanifa had said Amina was forbidden to go overseas, she explained. As the firstborn, America had been Oyin's birthright, and Esther had been charged by Orunmila to make it happen for the girl. But Esther could not. Or rather, she would not. She resented Temi for taking what belonged to her—her rightful place as the only woman in Sani's life, and as a result, Amina being the firstborn.

"I can't erase what my mother did. But maybe she has already paid for her sins. She certainly isn't here to talk about it." Oyin felt shame about her childhood, but defensive of Temi too. "And to tell you the truth, I envied Amina. Something that I wanted—that so many of us wanted—she accomplished, without letting anyone get in her way. I don't fault her."

"But be honest, Oyin, aren't you angry that you did not have that chance?"

"I don't really know. I mean, do you think things would be different if I had gone?"

"Regardless of what Temi did, I stole your future from you. And what happened to Amina, in the end, was my own fault."

"No, you can't do that to yourself. But you didn't answer my question. Do you wonder if Amina would still be alive, had I taken her place?"

"I don't know." Esther turned from Oyin, and her voice faded into itself.

"We are being honest, right?"

"We are, yes. Of course, I've thought about it. Amina being a child of this land, as was said—if she had stayed, she would not have died. I don't know what would have happened to you in America—I would never wish you harm, god knows that—but at least you would have been where you were destined to be. And the same for Amina."

"You should know"—the hardness in Oyin's chest loosened—"I like my life. No, there's no husband, no children."

"Yet." Esther reached for Oyin's arm.

"Maybe never! But I still like my life. And the thing is, there's no guarantee that listening to this prophet or that oracle or some god will spare any of us the pain of living. What about the hundreds of others in that city who perished in the same storm—did they all lose their way, miss a divine pronouncement? I can't live like that, thinking I'm doomed because I ignored some prophecy. I have to believe that when it's all said and done, nothing is carved in stone. Sometimes we're fortunate, sometimes we're not. Despite our hopes, affliction comes to us all the same."

Esther nodded throughout, though she was not ready to discard belief in preordainment just yet. And how could she, when a dream she hadn't even dreamed—Laila and Joseph in Nigeria—was coming true. Finally, she allowed herself to wonder aloud whether Laila was anything like Amina.

"If she is, it would serve us right," Oyin teased. She had been reveling in it—that she would now be an aunty, truly, not just in that Nigerian way, where every woman older than you is called one.

THE SHELLS HAVE SPOKEN. Oyin and Esther were relieved of a strain they hadn't known sat between them. Into this new opening, they shall welcome Laila.

IYANIFA: LAILA AND ESTHER

Shells in the shape of rest

LAILA AND JOSEPH SAT IN THE OPEN AIR, ON A DIRT road that had been converted into dining for a suya café. A young woman with the name of a beer company stamped on every inch of her shirt and slacks walked back and forth, in and out of an adjacent building, hoping someone would notice her and place an order.

"What is she like?" Laila asked.

"It's hard to say." Joseph straightened in his chair. "Her heart is kind, I'm sure of that. But life's been tough, you know? If you're worried, you don't need to be."

Laila shook her head, unassured. "I guess I don't know what she's expecting from me."

"I think you should talk about whatever's on your mind. Maybe you can tell her about your art, what you like to do in California. She will love you—I know it."

The plastic bag with the three envelopes addressed to Esther sat on the table, next to Laila's Fanta—her new favorite drink since she arrived. Until a few minutes ago, Laila had not told Joseph she'd brought the letters. She wondered if her grandmother would tell her what Amina had written. She hoped this meeting would go well.

"It'll be fine, you'll see."

Laila let go of the breath she had been holding. Joseph offered a certainty that, even if untrue, gave her the hope she sought.

They ate suya and waited for Esther.

With the a cappella on the outside speakers as a sentimental backdrop, Laila wondered if Amina, too, had sat in a place like this, eating and enjoying life.

"Who is that singing?" Laila asked Joseph.

"Salif Keita. From Mali."

"He sounds kind of sad."

"Yes, but beautiful too. Beauty and grief—that's life, huh?" Joseph smiled, pleased with himself for the pithy reflection.

Laila hoped not, since she still had years to live. She checked her phone to be sure they'd come to the right place. They had. She adjusted the drawstring of her dress, rubbed her lips together to be sure her lip gloss was evenly spread. It was.

Laila knew loss and feeling unwanted. She expected those things, even while convinced she was hopeful. Three minutes to the time they had agreed on, she sank into doubt: What if Esther had changed her mind about meeting her?

Several months ago, Laila had gone on her first blind date—a guy she had bantered with online, a friend of a friend. She'd sat at the coffee shop, watching the minutes fade until it was one hour past their meeting time. There is no feeling like it, waiting in a place and realizing the person for whom you have waited is not coming. After an hour more, after calling with no response, Laila left. She went home and cried. Sitting there, expecting Esther, her body remembered. She checked the time on her phone.

Laila looked up and there Esther was, on the horizon, walking toward them. She glided, more like, her blue kaftan flowing and sparkling with the sunlight. When she raised her arms, the dress spread outward like wings.

Laila stood. She hugged Esther, resting the side of her face on her grandmother's breasts; the smell of bergamot, plantains, and warm skin flowed through Esther's dress into Laila's breath. She wondered if this was mothering, having no memory of anything like it—not even with Aunty Fatima. Laila remained there, inhaling the scent—the arms that had cradled Amina now held her.

She searched Esther's face for a glimpse of Amina—she didn't see it. She found instead a hint of her own. Something minor that might never be noticed, except by the one seeking it. Under the bottom lip, Esther's mouth creased even when she smiled; a persistent, inherited sadness.

"Joseph told me all the places you've already been." Esther pulled her chair closer to Laila and asked how things were.

"I wanted to feel Mom's presence everywhere, but really," Laila shook her head, "I didn't."

Esther cupped Laila's chin. "What is it that you want to know?"

"If she's with me."

Esther and Joseph looked to each other for something to say.

"When Amina was about your age, there was this rock in our old neighborhood—she would sit there for hours." Esther had not returned to the rock in all this time. Remembering had been unbearable. "They say the rock gives answers—through the iyanifa that rests underneath."

"Aunty Fatima told me about it."

They would go to the rock together, the two women and Oyin, Joseph said.

"You will come as well, Joseph, no?" The more Esther was with Joseph, the more she wanted him around.

"Of course, if you'd like that," he said.

"I would like it," Esther said, looking straight into Joseph's eyes.

Joseph's body warmed.

"Oyin can't wait to meet you, you know," Esther said, turning back to Laila. "She's still settling in from her trip. We'll go to the rock the day after tomorrow."

"That's fine," Laila said. "I brought you these. I found them in a bag of Mom's things, a long time ago." She handed the three envelopes to Esther.

Esther knew Amina's handwriting. Her hands trembled. It had hurt that Amina didn't write as often as Esther did. And she rarely called. When the pain of Amina's death was unrelenting, Esther lay on her bedroom floor. *What I wouldn't give to hear my girl's voice again*, she would cry.

She held the letters to her chest.

ESTHER

Shells in the shape of sound

LAILA.

When you are feeling alone, may this letter bring you near to your mother.

⁓

AFTER JOSEPH CALLED AND said you were coming to Nigeria, I wrote to Amina for the last time. Joseph was my first love—the one that got away, as they say nowadays. And you, Laila, are the love I have missed. Nothing will replace Amina, no. But love, it seems, can be found anew—a surprise I am learning to understand. I woke up this morning, happy for every reason and no reason at all.

These have been my feelings, since you and Joseph came. Your presence would have been gift enough. So you can imagine my shock when I read the letters from Amina and discovered that all three were written in August 2005, right before the storm! It was as if she knew then that she was living her final days.

In the first letter, there are two photos: a studio one of you as a newborn, curled up inside a wicker basket; another of you standing in your crib, your face poking through the slats. *I can't wait for you to meet Laila!* she wrote.

Then there is the letter about Joseph: Amina said she had seen him one day, on the way out of her favorite café. At the end, she included his number and address. *His eyes light up at the mention of your name*, she wrote. *Mummy, I think you should get in touch. He is such a nice man.* She wrote these letters and put them away. I can only think they were for me to have, now.

But the letter that nearly shattered me is the third one. She shared parts of herself that I never knew. She was reading stories, she said, by African women. She loved coffee and thin-crust pizza. She practiced yoga in her bedroom, at night, after you, Fatima, and Rashid had gone to sleep. She was good at it and wanted to take a class. She could have been one of the writers she mentioned, Laila—so rich were her descriptions of her last days. And she said this, that I cannot forget: *I wish I had asked more about the things you loved, before me.* She had been thinking of me.

I was awake late last night, after leaving you and Joseph. I read each of the three letters again and thought of you, Laila. My dear, don't you worry. You, too, will become—in the absence of your mother. You will have new and secret loves at which you will excel. You will make her proud, even if she is not there to see. But I will see, Laila. I am here. And we, the women before you, are with you wherever you go.

IYANIFA: THE FIVE OF THEM

Shells in the shape of remembering

LAILA CLOSED THE HOTEL ROOM DOOR AND WALKED down to the lobby.

Esther sat on a sofa by the beveled-glass window. The younger woman next to Esther—about the age Amina would be now—could only be Oyin, Laila thought. The two women spotted Laila and floated over, cooing over everything straightaway, as if she had been a part of them long lost and now returned. Laila did not retreat.

Esther hugged her granddaughter and put the letter inside Laila's handbag. "For you, my dear."

"Joseph is out front." Oyin, with the curved tips of her fabulous nails, swept waist-length braids behind her ears and shimmied. "If I'm going to sit on some rock, I will look my best, abi. Some of the finest single daddies in Ibadan frequent that area."

Laila giggled.

Esther shook her head, smiling. "Don't mind her, Laila." She walked slowly behind the two girls, gathering and gathering again the hem of her lace shoulder wrap as they stepped out into the wind. In the light of day, she watched Laila's feet for the measure of dust. There was a clear print on the ground. Esther breathed, relieved.

"I told you everything would be all right," Joseph whispered to Laila as she settled into the front seat of the car.

So that was what the women did, head to Eternal Rock. Windows down and Joseph driving, a different kind of silence filled their midst.

Driving up to the rock, Joseph explained its name to Laila, differentiating between the two Yoruba words used. Esther and Oyin sat in the back, listening and nodding along. Joseph parked the car on the outer edge of the roundabout. The women locked their handbags in the trunk.

They sat on the rock. Joseph's arm around Esther, Oyin and Laila watching the morning's unfolding, and Amina's spirit between them, this was the closest the five had been since they held hands at Imole. As above, Sani lags behind, somewhere out of reach.

Only god can determine the end, from the beginning—at most, humans imagine what is to come. In our living, when the time ahead is less than what is behind, can we sense it? It could be that Amina's soul reached for America—Oyin's birthright be damned—to give herself a chance to become something new, in the most tremendous way. About the three women on this rock, gathered in her honor—her beginning, middle, and an unexpected end—she might say the love she sought in leaving had been with her where she began. One way or another, the children of the land must return home.

IYANIFA: JOSEPH AND ESTHER

Shells in the shape of becoming

BY THE TIME JOSEPH AND ESTHER RETURNED FROM THE rock, chatter had spread through Felicity Lane, Esther's new neighborhood:

"Ah, so they are finally together!"

"Sixty-something? What could they possibly want at that age?"

"He patted her backside out in the open—they were shameless, O!"

"I hear he is a dish boy at her restaurant now."

Joseph had brought back their love child—Laila—who had been living with him in America, one stream of gossip claimed.

But when did Esther go abroad to have a baby with Joseph? When the gossiper was pressed on this point, "Does it really matter?" was the response.

⌒

ESTHER AND JOSEPH SAT at a table in the back of the restaurant.

In the middle of the main dining room, Amina's ankara head wrap adorned the wall. It was already in the shape of a rectangle, so Esther had ironed and centered the cloth on a canvas frame; she enclosed it in glass. A small placard next to it read simply *Amina*. Just yesterday, several customers had asked about the meaning of the cloth artwork. This gave Esther the chance to tell Amina's story.

Amina's one choice—America—had been devastating for those who loved her, but had also enlarged their lives, through Laila. American by birth and free to move within and between worlds, Laila has feet now in places Amina only dreamed of. That which was for her mother the zenith of achievement is for Laila the beginning of all she can become.

"I want her with me—here," Esther had said, when she showed the framed ankara to Joseph.

He had wrapped his arm around Esther and assured her it was a lovely tribute.

This evening, the waitstaff swept and straightened up around them. Tap water ran in the kitchen sink. The last customers, a father and his lively little boys, bounced out the door.

Joseph reached across the table for Esther's hands. "If I stay, what would I do?" He had been decades out of the engineering loop. At his age, it was near impossible to start anew—not without a connection. He had enough dollars to last him some time, sure, but he wanted to feel useful.

In our culture, a man does not put himself in the supporting role of his woman's business. Joseph needed his own thing. And yet he enjoyed how he and Esther worked together. He'd spent much of his free time the last two weeks helping her with bulk orders and payroll. Yesterday, he called the airline and made his return ticket open-ended. He was prepared to stay.

"We can change the sign on the door to *Esther and Joseph's*." Esther winked, hoping to lighten the heaviness that could arise from the conversation. "In all seriousness, I could use some help here. If things go well, we'll retire—maybe to America, to keep an eye on Laila."

Joseph laughed.

Esther was not concerned. She wasn't a wealthy woman that Joseph could fleece, regardless of what the gossipers predicted. If they could work together on the restaurant, she would welcome it. If he chose something else, she would be all right with that too. More than anything, Esther wanted Joseph to stay.

"Let me think about it," he said. He couldn't hold back; he took Esther's fingers to his lips. She held his face and pulled him in. Neither cared about the eyes around them. And the staff didn't mind the open display. Esther's freeness, these last few weeks, had enlivened the atmosphere, filling all with the hope that it is never too late.

IYANIFA: LAILA

Shells in the shape of a return

A WEEK AFTER RETURNING TO CALIFORNIA, LAILA cocooned inside the memory of a place she could now claim. On the plane ride back, the woman next to her had asked what she'd been doing in Nigeria, all by herself.

"Visiting my family," she'd said—a response that surprised even her. She felt as if she belonged to them now: Esther, Joseph, and Oyin.

At the boutique, the unacknowledged silence between Laila and Fatima remained.

"What will you do now?" Fatima had asked, finally, yesterday afternoon.

"I'm still thinking about it."

"You know you always have my help, if you need it."

Laila did not want to need Fatima's help. She only wanted more time, to decide what to do next. Earlier that morning, she had signed up for an information session at an art institute in their town. Laila had options. "I know. Thank you," she said.

LAILA TOOK HER TIME, walking to the café. An hour ago, she'd sent a text message to Tosin—to accept his offer of discussing home. She was ready, now, to talk. She'd memorized the necessary facts about the Nigerian government and current fads. Just enough political and social trivia to lean the conversation her way. And, too, she needed someone to tell about her family.

Hey there. I know it's been a while. I just came back from Nigeria. Can you believe it? You wanna meet up for coffee? It's Laila, by the way.

Ten minutes later, Tosin wrote back: *Laila! Yeah, sure. I'm in the area now. Meet in an hour?*

She would wear jeans and a T-shirt—casual, so he wouldn't think she tried too hard. She had not had a pedicure in weeks, but with peep-toe sandals, she could get away with that.

Laila was one block from the café when Tosin wrote again: *I'm like two minutes away. Don't get coffee without me. My treat!*

Earlier this morning, Laila had talked to Joseph—a static-laced, shouting call with one of the latest phone applications.

"Oh yes, I'm certain," he responded, when she asked about his decision to stay. "You know, I'm enjoying helping Esther run the restaurant. Besides, what would I be doing over there, at my age? I can't tempt fate twice." He was full of cheer.

No one thought it would end this way for Joseph and Esther, though Amina had hoped it. Some might say it was because of their old age. Maybe it was in spite of it.

"I'm happy for you," Laila said. "And grandma."

Grandma. It had taken several tries to decide what she would call Esther, who had left it up to her. *Grandmother* felt too formal; admittedly, *grandma* had a familiarity they had just begun to earn. But as with everything else, Laila was learning to give things the room they needed to evolve.

She entered the café and there Tosin was—having gotten there first—waiting for her.

IYANIFA: AARIN

THE SHELLS TELL ME SO.
None of the family Amina knew awaited her return, after her ascent. Their lives carried on, new joys and sufferings on their horizons. Olodu was there, after her rest. In the fleeting void that followed, Esther and Laila appeared to her, as in a dream; at their meeting, Amina was relieved.

Now she must decide the way to go.

Imole, the brilliant edge, provides one solace: forgetting it all. Here, the past is like a bruise, the cause of which cannot be recalled. When it heals, there is an aching so profound.

Aarin, the middle place, offers the chance to remember, in order that we might guide and warn. I know, because the middle place is what I, Iyanifa, Ifa priestess, mother of mysteries, diviner of Orunmila, chose. I watch over the children, above and below. Maybe Amina will join me, never having been this way before. Time has no borders here—she has yet to decide.

A NOTE ON YORUBA DIACRITICAL MARKS

YORUBA, IN WRITTEN FORM, uses diacritical marks to denote its primary classification as a tonal language—one in which a single word can have multiple meanings, depending on the tone(s) employed. The correct tone, signaling the intended meaning of the Yoruba word, is indicated by the use of certain marks on vowels. In addition to tone marks on vowels, written Yoruba also uses diacritical marks on consonants to signify a post-alveolar sound, for example.

In this novel, I have chosen to write Yoruba words without their diacritical marks—tonal and other—in order to accurately reflect my own modest knowledge of the use of these marks. Although I learned Yoruba as a first language, can speak and read it fluently, and can write it to some degree, as an adult who has primarily spoken, read, and written in the English language since age eight when I emigrated from Nigeria to the US, I do not know how to use diacritical marks as well as I would like. As a first-generation African and American child of Nigerian parents, the movement between native and acquired language, ancestral and birthplace culture, home and outside vernacular has meant that my most genuine expression of Yoruba is likewise in-between. This dynamic position that I— and some of the characters in *The Edge of Water*—inhabit is one I have come to embrace.

A NOTE ON HISTORICAL ACCURACY

THIS NOVEL IS CENTERED on the real-life Hurricane Katrina, which made landfall near New Orleans, Louisiana, on August 29, 2005. Though the novel draws upon many of the realities of the event, I have also intentionally diverged from some of the historical details to best fit this story and these characters.

CREDITS

I WANT TO EXPRESS my heartfelt gratitude to the following literary journals and their wonderful editors and staff for publishing my short stories, in which parts of this novel first appeared: *Michigan Quarterly Review* ("Aminatu"), *Glimmer Train* ("26 Bones"), *Ploughshares* ("Serrated"), AGNI ("The Spirit of Entitlement"), *New Letters* ("Slighted"), *The Antioch Review* ("Unaddressed"), and *Stand Magazine* ("Talk on Elekuro Street").

REFERENCES

p. 30: The song referenced here is Marvin Gaye's "Sexual Healing" from his 1982 album *Midnight Love*.

p. 223: Joan Rivers is the comedian who, in 2002, made the observation in her comedy special "Look Good" (part of the *Just for Laughs* comedy festival held in Montreal, Canada) that older men's testicles over a commode are like teabags dipped in a cup of water.

p. 224: Kahlil Gibran, in *The Prophet* (Alfred A. Knopf, 1923), made the observation about the origin and destiny of children.

ACKNOWLEDGMENTS

MY DREAM OF THIS NOVEL has been nearly twenty years in coming true.

I have learned that the right literary agent matters to the possibilities of a book; this novel would not be what it is without the unwavering dedication of the magnificent Danya Kukafka, who believed in me and my work immediately, and then gave me the years and encouragement I needed to write this story, from beginning to end. I could go on about your brilliance, contagious enthusiasm, and the gift you have been to me throughout. Thank you for everything.

The right editor absolutely matters not only to a book's outcome, but also to a writer's well-being during the course of publication; I am so fortunate to have landed with the incredibly talented, attentive, thoughtful, and consistently kind and generous Elizabeth DeMeo. I am forever grateful that you embraced this story and loved these characters as you have. I am joyous for our work together! Thank you.

The right publisher matters to the reputation of a book; I am proud to debut as a Tin House author. Their excellence precedes them, and the excitement and warmth with which they have embraced this novel and me are more than I hoped for. I thank every person who worked on *The Edge of Water* at every stage—especially Elizabeth DeMeo, Masie Cochran,

Becky Kraemer, Nanci McCloskey, Jacqui Reiko Teruya, Jae Nichelle, Beth Steidle, Mariah Rigg, Allison Dubinsky, and Lisa Dusenbery. Thank you.

MY DEEP GRATITUDE TO:

The late, esteemed Laurence Goldstein, who enthusiastically published my first short story (the one upon which this novel is based) in *Michigan Quarterly Review*. Linda B. Swanson-Davies of *Glimmer Train*, who has remained a friend of my work through the years. All the editors of the journals that published my short stories. Thank you.

The organizations that have supported my work by providing time, money, and critical encouragement: Literary Arts in Portland, Oregon; Bread Loaf Writers' Conference; The Rona Jaffe Foundation; Ludwig Vogelstein Foundation; and Voices of Our Nations Arts Foundation (VONA). All my workshop teachers, especially ZZ Packer, David Mura, and Chang-rae Lee. Jami Attenberg, Maurice Carlos Ruffin, and Vanessa Walters for your great generosity in making time for an early read of the novel; your praise means the world. Thank you.

Trellis Literary Management for your expansive vision, and dedication to your clients—thank you.

Those who believed in me, when I shared my writing dreams: Kristina S., Stacy-Ann, Mary S., Amy P., Kathy M., Janekka, Juliana and her family, Olumide, Indira and Kimi, Rochelle R., Kris and Owen, Tobin, Kim and Simon, Whitney, Kennedy, Tim and Becky, Tony and Melissa, Jennifer and Amin, Dalia, Rachel and Kai, Susan M., and others unnamed. Thank you.

The teachers I'm unable to forget: Mr. Caroscio, Ms. Holmes, Ms. Pedone, Mr. Bain, Professor Harcourt, Professor Washington. I hope you see this—and thank you.

The places I have lived and loved: Ibadan, New Orleans, and the San Francisco Bay Area especially. The people and things there that have inspired parts of the novel: Mama Jennifer, Vera Williams, and the Community Book Center family; Leola and others unnamed; all my favorite cafés and their tasty, fueling coffee. The feelings that deepen my remembering—thank you.

High Chief Simeon Olaleye Orisagbemi Oginni (the Alaye of Ijesaland), the Obatala priest who helped me understand more deeply the formal aspects of Ifa, the religion of my paternal ancestors. Ranti Ajeleti, Esq., for kindly facilitating our meeting. Thank you.

The African writers on whose shoulders I stand: The late, incomparable Yvonne Vera, who employed language like no one else. The late Mariama Bâ, whose stunning *So Long A Letter* inspired the epistolary structure between Esther and Amina. Tsitsi Dangarembga, for *Nervous Conditions* and her notable kindness. Many other African writers, unnamed. The larger writing community, from which I continually receive inspiration and comfort that I am not alone on this wondrous and trying journey. And you, dear reader. Thank you.

The friends who in various ways helped me, so I could keep writing: Ms. Amy, Linda A., Clare K., Samira F., Laila, Kat and Matt, and others unnamed. Thank you.

My godmother, who read the *Ramona* series with me—which helped spark my love for books. Thank you.

My ancestors in every world. My family of origin, especially my mother, Adenike Adejumo, who told the juiciest stories while I eavesdropped from wherever I could, and who, for me, is the embodiment of Yoruba. Thank you.

Jonah, Tayo, Dele—with whom I'm living the life I once dreamed. Thank you.

1. Esther, Amina, and—to a smaller extent—Iyanifa are the only characters who directly tell their own stories. Why do you think the author chose these characters? Are there other characters you'd be curious to hear from?

2. Grappling with regret is a recurring theme in the novel; how does each character reckon with this feeling by the end of the book?

3. Dreams—in sleep and waking, expressed and silent—feature prominently throughout the novel, especially for Esther and Amina. How does Laila embody her mother's and grandmother's unspoken dreams?

4. From the start of the novel, Esther talks to Amina in the form of letters, though Amina does not address Esther directly until much later. Why do you think the author made this decision?

5. Amina tells us that her desire to be free—of everyone, even Esther—makes her feel disinherited from her Africanness. How does the theme of disinheritance weave throughout the various relationships in the novel?

6. Amina's neighborhoods in Ibadan are markedly similar to *and* different from her neighborhood in New Orleans. How did her years in Nigeria prepare her for America?

7. What hints might Laila and Tosin's burgeoning relationship provide about their lives before or to come?

8. What will Amina choose, Imole or Aarin? Where in the novel might you find clues to support your prediction?

9. Despite the devastation of the storm at the center of the novel, there are also moments of levity and joy throughout—which most resonated with you and why?

10. At the beginning of the novel, the author tells us, "A storm is coming." Aside from the hurricane, what other storms do we encounter in the book?

MALAK YASSIN

OLUFUNKE GRACE BANKOLE

is a Nigerian American writer. A graduate of Harvard Law School and a recipient of a Soros Justice Advocacy Fellowship, her work has appeared in various literary journals, including *Ploughshares*, *Glimmer Train*, *AGNI*, *Michigan Quarterly Review*, *New Letters*, the *Antioch Review*, and *Stand*. She won the first-place prize in the *Glimmer Train* Short Story Award for New Writers, and was the Bread Loaf-Rona Jaffe Scholar in Fiction at the Bread Loaf Writers' Conference. She has been awarded an Oregon Literary Fellowship in Fiction, a Ludwig Vogelstein Foundation grant, a residency-fellowship from the Anderson Center at Tower View, and has received a Pushcart Special Mention for her writing. She lives in Portland, Oregon.